Hearts
in the
Sand

by Jennifer L. Allen

I0461042

Hearts in the Sand

Copyright © 2016 Jennifer L. Allen

All rights reserved.

Published: Jennifer L. Allen 2016

jenniferlallenauthor@gmail.com

Editor: Aimee Lukas
Cover Design: Pink Ink Designs

Dedication

This one is for the readers.
You wanted more of the boys from JACT.
Here they are.
Thank you for enjoying it enough to ask for more!
And thank you for giving me a reason to revisit
these guys, I had fun.

A Special Shout-Out
to the Readers
Who Asked For More!!

Thank you! Thank you for reading *Our Moon* and for loving the guys of JACT so much that you asked for more. *Our Moon* was meant to be a standalone. I had no intentions of adding more stories. Ask any of my betas and early reviewers – I was adamant that it was all by itself! But some of you fell in love with the other guys in JACT and wanted to learn more about them, so I decided that if a story came to me that suited those characters, I'd write it. I had no particular order in mind, no ideas at all really, just a general sense of what these guys were like. I started working on a short story for Joey and Evie, which seemed pretty simple. Since their story was already told in *Our Moon*, I only had to fill in the gaps and make it interesting. Naturally, I hit a wall with that book. I wasn't quite sure where to take it and didn't want to disappoint everyone and fill it with crap, so I set it aside to write *Change of Heart*, because that story was screaming at me in my head. *Hearts in the Sand* came to me while I was vacationing in the Outer Banks last summer, finishing up *Change of Heart*. I started getting ideas for a vacation romance and was prepared to write something brand new when it dawned on me...the guys in JACT can take a vacation, right? Pieces started to fall into place and I realized that *this* was Trevor's book. He and the female lead I drew up in my mind meshed so well together. It was perfect. As soon as

Change of Heart went to edit, I started pouring this story out. It was speaking to me so clearly and I couldn't stop writing. And here you have it! I have every intention of returning to Joey and Evie soon. I even have a little idea brewing for Alex. I'm hoping to be able to share those stories with you next year. In the meantime, I've got a couple other projects brewing and I don't think you'll be disappointed. Thank you again for your support and your love for these characters. I hope you enjoy!!

Chapter One

Trevor

"Vacation, all I ever wanted..."

"Vacation, had to get away..."

"Vacation, meant to be spent ALONE!"

"Alex!" my sister, Ally, and Joey's wife, Evie, both shout from the third row. The rest of us laugh. It was only a matter of time before someone put a stop to their off-key renditions of every 80s girl rock song imaginable. I don't know about anyone else, but being trapped in a vehicle with the two of them singing had been grating on my nerves the last couple hours.

"Al, who is the lead singer of the band?" Alex asks. Tapping his chin with his index finger, he turns to look over his seat and patiently waits for her response.

"I'm not in the band," she says, crossing her arms over her chest and lifting her chin in defiance.

"Al...who is the singer?"

Eventually she sighs, knowing better than anyone that Alex isn't going to stop until she answers. "You are."

"So doesn't it make sense that if anyone is going to be singing, it should be me?"

Evie laughs. "Right, like last night?" The rest of us join in the laughter, remembering Alex's excitement last night as the hours counted down to our first family vacation in years.

Alex rolls his eyes and faces forward. "Everyone likes Eddie Money." He crosses his arms over his chest and lifts his chin in a move nearly identical to the one his twin had performed a moment ago. Alex and Ally are fraternal twins and as different as night and day in most regards, but many of their mannerisms are the same.

"Pretty sure Eddie had 'two tickets to paradise,' not six and a half," Joey says, nudging Alex's arm across the small aisle with his elbow.

"Uh yeah...there are six and a half of us," Alex argues as if it makes all the sense in the world, the 'half' being Max, Joey and Evie's three-year-old son. We all laugh again at the seriousness of his expression. "Whatever, you guys all suck."

"Why so down brother?" Ally leans forward, between Joey and Alex's seats. "You were so excited last night."

"That was before I realized our mode of transportation for this much anticipated trip was a minivan," he whines.

Ally giggles, a sound I'll never get tired of hearing. The night of the twins' high school graduation, five years ago, she and our parents were in a car accident. Our parents didn't make it and Ally spent a year in a coma. When she finally woke up, she'd had amnesia. After more than three years of no memories, they'd finally come back about ten months ago, so catching these glimpses of the old, relaxed Ally never ceases to bring a smile to my face.

"It's the only thing that would fit all of us," Evie reminds Alex.

"How about a limo?"

"You don't take a limo to the beach, Alex," Evie says, shaking her head.

"We could have gotten one of those cool Hummer limos." I roll my eyes; it's not the first time Alex has suggested a Hummer limo.

"It's just not practical," Evie says, reading my mind.

"We're rock stars! We're not supposed to be practical!" Ally shakes her head at Alex's outburst, and leans back in her seat.

Alex, Joey, Chase and I are in a rock band. We formed JACT—named for the first letters of each of our names—in my parents' garage back in high school. Alex sings, Joey plays drums, Chase is on guitar, and I play bass. We got signed when Ally was in the coma, had a very successful first tour, and things just took off for us after that. Now our music is everywhere, though it's still surreal to hear our songs on the radio.

"How'd y'all find this place on such short notice anyway?" Ally asks, attempting to steer the conversation away from Alex's complaining.

"Humph said someone owed him a favor," I told her.

Humph, a.k.a. Humphrey Morris, is one of the execs at our label who had taken an immediate liking to us. The suits at labels didn't usually spend too much time with the talent but Humph was different. Probably because we were different. He took us under his wing like the kids he never had, and we accepted him as sort of the parental figure we no longer had. It was nice to have someone looking out for us in that way again since mine and Alex's parents had died and Joey and Chase's parents don't deserve the title.

"That's awesome, I can't wait to see it."

***

Awesome had been an understatement. The house is practically a palace. It's three floors with white siding, black shutters and wrap around decks on each level. Our house back in Charlotte is a pretty decent size, but this place is huge. The best part? It's only minutes from the beach—just a golf cart ride away.

Alex, Ally and I had gone to the Outer Banks of North Carolina with our parents once when we were kids. It was so long ago that none of us remember it well, but it was the first place we thought of when deciding where to take a month off this summer. I think we all secretly hope being here will bring back our memories of having been here with our mom and dad—bring us closer to them in some way.

I grab the last few bags out of the back of the van and follow the rest of the group up the wooden staircase to the front door. Chase uses the four-digit code Humph gave us to unlock the wide door and swings it open. We enter between the first and second floors and make our way up the hardwood staircase, knowing the bedrooms are on the second and third levels.

The second floor opens to a lounge area complete with overstuffed couches and a wall-mounted flat screen TV. Alex takes the first room on the left, and I take the one beside him, both are complete master suites. Chase and Ally take one of the suites on the right side. It's still a little weird that my best friend is dating—correction, engaged to—my baby sister, but if I had to choose anyone for Ally, it would be Chase. Over the past few years, he's shown unrelenting dedication to her and a ridiculous amount of patience. If that's not love, I don't know what is.

We had agreed ahead of time that Joey and Evie would get the largest suite on the third floor since they needed the extra space for Max, so after setting our things down, we help them lug their things upstairs. Aside from the bedroom, the third floor is completely open, holding the kitchen and a large living room. The same light colored hardwood that makes up the staircase is spread wall-to-wall up here. The view is amazing. The entire back side of the house is windows with a clear view straight to the ocean beyond the deck. We can even see beachgoers laid out on blankets and towels. The beach is dotted with umbrellas and volleyball games at least a mile in each direction.

"This is amazing," Ally says, bumping my shoulder.

"It is." I put my arm around her shoulder and pull her into my side. "I bet you're just itching to get out there," I say, tipping my chin in the direction of the ocean. Ally was a swimmer back in high school; she'd won tons of competitions and her team made it to the state championship. She still gets in the water as much as she can.

I feel her shiver. "Oh no. I'll be content right down there in the pool," she says, pointing at the saltwater pool in the backyard. "I don't do dark water."

"Oh, come on," I tease. "You can outswim any shark out there."

"I'd rather not test that theory." She smiles at me. "Evie and I are about to make a shopping list so we can head to the grocery store, any requests?"

She asks me, but Alex yells "Beer!" from somewhere in the house. We're not big drinkers, but it *is* vacation.

"I swear he has ears like a dog." Ally grumbles, and I laugh, because so does she.

"You love me!" is his response and we both shake our heads.

"Anything you guys get will be fine. I've missed your cooking."

Ally beams and kisses me on the cheek before skipping over to the counter where Evie is sitting with a notepad. Since Ally graduated culinary school last year, I haven't been able to sample her food magic nearly as often as I'd like. She'd found work at a bakery immediately after graduation and has been extremely busy ever since.

"Remember...this is your vacation too, Al. You don't have to cook every night." I call over to her, and she sticks her tongue out in return. I laugh and shake my head, returning my gaze to the sea.

We've all been busy. The guys and I have been on tour and in the studio almost nonstop since we signed with the label. Evie joins us on tour when she and Max can, but Ally hasn't had the flexibility due to school and work. Now that she and Chase live in an apartment downtown, and Joey and Evie are busy with Max, we don't have the opportunity to see each other as much as we used to.

That's what this trip is about. The guys and I have a month—an entire month—where we don't have to go into the studio or play any shows, so we'd coerced Ally into taking time off for a vacation. We have a whole month to sit back, relax, and enjoy each other's company without having to run off to deal with our other responsibilities.

It's going to be great. I can only hope it won't be over before we realize it.

Chapter Two

Trevor

"This one does a tour of multiple lighthouses, a wild horse tour, and it even does restaurant tours," Evie says, looking over one of the travel brochures she and Ally picked up at the grocery store.

"Lemme see that." Ally reaches across the wide dining table and snatches it from her, her interest peaked at the idea of a restaurant tour.

At everyone's insistence—everyone except Ally—dinner tonight was takeout. After the travel, unpacking, and shopping, we needed tonight to relax. Ally had insisted that cooking soothes her, and it took Chase whispering something in her ear—something I don't ever want to know—to get her to back down. So here we sit amongst our dirty plates, piled high with empty crab legs and shells, shrimp tails and corn cob carcasses, checking out all there is to do in the Outer Banks.

"I'd like to see the Wright Brothers' Memorial," Chase says, waving the flyer.

"This one goes there," Ally tells him without looking up, her complete focus on the contents of the brochure in front of her.

"We definitely need to get some jet skis," Alex adds grinning. He and Joey high five, and for a brief moment, I worry about anyone else on the water that day.

"This one rents out jet skis, too."

"And parasailing," Joey says, grinning wider.

"Yep," Ally confirms.

"Is there anything they don't do?" Joey asks, leaning his elbow on Ally's shoulder.

"Sure doesn't seem like it. Don't forget you boys are on clean-up duty," Ally reminds us, an unspoken threat is clearly implied in her tone.

"Yeah, yeah," Alex replies, still looking over a flyer with various motorsports. "We should totally get a speedboat."

Like Chase and I are best friends, so are Alex and Joey. They're the same age and have the same carefree and easygoing attitudes, the opposite of Chase's and my more serious demeanors. Wild doesn't even begin to describe how the two of them can get when left to their own devices.

"Yeah, we can get a speedboat if Chase or Trevor drive it," Evie says.

"Babe?" Joey calls, his head popping up from behind the couch in the living room, an incredulous expression on his face. "What the heck?"

"If you think I'm gettin' in a *speed*boat with you or Tweedle Dee here behind the wheel," she hooks a thumb at Alex, "you've got another thing comin'." The way Evie's Texas twang comes out when she's making a point brings a smile to my face.

"Dee? *He's* Tweedle Dee? That means I'm Tweedle Dum. That's so not cool, babe."

"That's what he took from all that?" Ally mumbles, causing Evie, Chase, and I to laugh, and Alex to look at us with a confused expression. I'd say he's having a blond moment, but since he and Ally share the same sandy shade, she'll probably take offense and, while she's the more reserved twin, she can be quite the little pistol when she gets fired up—especially after a couple glasses of wine like the ones she and Evie had at dinner.

"So what do we have?" I ask, sitting back down after Chase and I clear off the table. I'm trying to tune out the ruckus that's happening in the kitchen behind me, where Joey and Alex are supposed to be rinsing dishes and loading the dishwasher. I have a feeling they're wetting down the entire kitchen.

Ally hands me the brochure for a company called Sand Tours. "They do pretty much everything we want to do, except the speedboat rental and golf–mini or full-size." I skim the pages and nod, seeing nearly everything there is to do from Hatteras to Corolla listed on its pages along with gorgeous images of the beach, grasslands, and wildlife.

"Looks good. I'll give them a call tomorrow."

"Maybe they have packages or something," Ally offers, always thinking frugally despite the fact that we're all pretty well off now. We could have lived comfortably off our inheritances alone for several years without even touching the band money.

"I'll check, kid," I say and she smiles at the nickname.

"How about we play a game after my kid goes to sleep?" Evie asks, returning from the living room where Max is curled up with a movie on his portable DVD player.

"Joey or Max?" Chase wonders.

Evie laughs. "Good question," she rolls her eyes and gestures towards Alex and Joey, both soaking wet and doing a walk of shame from the sink, realizing they've been caught.

"You'd better clean up the floor," I tell them, betting there are puddles all over the hardwood.

"I don't think they got any on the floor, Trev," Chase says as he takes them in. They are completely drenched from head to toe. "You know there's a pool out back? And the ocean?"

"Where are the towels?" Alex asks, ignoring Chase.

"First floor," Evie tells him.

As Alex and Joey take off down the stairs, Ally says "You do know we're probably not going to see them again tonight, right?"

It's a pretty fair assumption that Joey and Alex will remain on the ground floor for the rest of the evening since that's where the beer, foosball and pool tables are. Not to mention the pool just outside the sliding doors.

Ally's statement may as well have been punctuated by the large splash heard all around the house.

"Splash! Pool! Momma, pool?" Max, who was near sleep a few moments ago, is bouncing around the living room at the idea of someone splashing in the pool.

Evie's head thumps against the table with a groan. "God, grant me the serenity..." she trails off as she rises and makes her way to the living room and a now hyperactive Max. "Let's go see what dada's doing, kiddo!" She picks him up and swings him around, then goes down the stairs, Max babbling about the pool and dada and splash the entire way.

"Well, then," Ally says.

"If you can't beat 'em..." Chase starts.

"Join 'em," I complete his thought, with a smirk.

Chase grins and Ally laughs as we get up from the table and run down the stairs, shedding wallets and cell phones along the way. We run straight out the still open sliding glass doors and cannonball into the pool.

When we surface, Evie is standing on the pool deck, soaking wet from the splash, shaking her head, while Max is bouncing in her arms saying "again, again." Joey and Alex are making their way around the pool, high-fiving us.

"The Tweedles, yes," Evie says, referring to Joey and Alex. "But I didn't expect this from the three of you."

"We're on vacation," Ally shouts, splashing the water beside her.

"Vacation!" Joey and Alex chorus.

"Get in the pool, Evie," Ally says.

"Y'all are crazy! I'm not in my bathing suit and neither is Max."

"Gimme my kid!" Joey calls out, swimming to the side of the pool by Evie.

"No," she says, taking a step back.

"Dada! Swim! Pool!"

"See? He wants to swim," Joey says, giving her his best smile.

"Oh, fine! For the love of all that is holy. It's so past his bedtime, Joseph." Evie mutters as she squats down and hands Max over to Joey, who passes him off to Ally before pulling Evie into the pool. "Joseph!"

Max says, "Momma all wet!" and we all laugh, even Evie.

Yep, I think to myself as I float on my back listening to the laughter and banter of my family, this is exactly what we needed.

Chapter Three

Trevor

Three days into our trip and I've made reservations for a private wild horse tour near Corolla, on the northern end of the Outer Banks. In a place like this, it's not likely we'd be recognized, but just in case—I'd rather not get stuck in a vehicle with the only screaming fan in the area.

Sand Tours is a good thirty minutes from our rental and since we need to arrive early to sign waivers, we leave an hour before our eleven o'clock tour. Alex calls shotgun and mumbles about wanting to rent his own Jeep the entire drive while I do my best to ignore him. Chase and Ally sit in the middle club seats, holding hands and sharing the occasional goo-goo eyes. Joey and Evie sit in the third row fielding questions from Max about the horses, driving on the beach, and anything else he sees out the window.

"Sitting up here, I can almost pretend I'm not in a mom van," Alex snarks from beside me.

"Dude, it's not that big of a deal."

"Not that big of a deal?" he scoffs. "How am I gonna attract any fine females with this ride?"

"Shouldn't you be more concerned about the 'fine females' being attracted to you as a person?" Ally asks.

Alex thinks about it for a moment. "No, not really. I mean who's *not* attracted to me? That part's a given. But when I escort them out to my vehicle and they see it's a mom-mobile...that'll be where my night ends."

Ally shakes her head, "So superficial."

"That's what I'm looking for, Al." Alex states matter-of-factly. "I want to find a nice superficial girl because I know she'll take care of herself and make a perfect future trophy wife."

"Are you being serious right now?" I interject. Alex has always been a tad bit on the wild side, and a bit of an airhead, but I find it hard to believe he's scouting out candidates for a trophy wife.

"As a heart attack."

"I'm not superficial," Ally says with a little heat in her tone, "does that mean I'm not good enough to be on Chase's arm? What about Evie, huh? She's not superficial either."

"It's different for Chase and Joey, they're in the background. I'm the lead singer. I'm front and center. I'm what everyone sees. Fans and the media have higher expectations for me."

The sad thing about it is that Alex has no idea the hole he's just dug himself and judging by the increased redness of my sister's face in the rear view mirror, it's about to get nuclear up in this mom-mobile.

"I'm not even sure what to address first here, *Alexander*. The fact that you think you're more important than everyone else in the band, or that you're suggesting it's okay for Evie and I to be unattractive, or at least less attractive than your arm-candy."

Alex's eyes widen a smidge at Ally's tone and her use of his full name. Good, hopefully some sense is sinking into his thick skull.

"Course I don't think you're unattractive, Al. You're my twin, that's just not possible."

Through the rear view mirror, I see Chase whispering in Ally's ear, and a small smile graces her face as her shoulders relax. Whatever he'd said soothes her enough that she no longer questions Alex's nonsense. The rest of us have been stuck in a bus on tour together long enough to know: Do Not Engage. It's our mantra most of the time. Since Ally hasn't joined us for a full tour yet, she doesn't realize this is all just par for the course with her twin. Half the time he doesn't even mean what he says, he's just looking for a reaction.

Fortunately, I see the sign up ahead for Sand Tours and make a right into the parking lot, effectively putting an end to more crap coming from Alex's mouth...at least for the time being. Sand Tours is in a free-standing, sand-colored building. The sign is ocean blue with the "Sand Tours" logo in white lettering, riding the top of a wave. There are several off-road vehicles in the parking lot, and in the back I can see colorful kayaks, ATVs and jet skis loaded on trailers. They really are a one-stop-shop. The parking lot is pretty packed, but I find a spot for the mom-mobile. What can I say? The name kind of stuck.

"It's a good thing we made a reservation," Evie says from the back, taking in the pedestrian traffic in the parking lot.

"Yeah, they seem pretty popular. Guess it was a good choice of place," Ally adds.

"I'll go check in while you all unload," I tell them before I make my way across the lot to the front door. The sun beats down and I silently thank myself for making sure our vehicle had a roof when I made the reservation. Initially I'd been concerned about privacy, now I'm concerned about the sun. I hope the girls brought some high SPF, Lord knows none of us guys are smart enough to think of it.

I open the door and step aside to let a group of teenagers through. I'm glad I'm wearing my sunglasses and ball cap since one of them has a JACT t-shirt on. I smile; seeing people wearing our merchandise or listening to our music never gets old. Hopefully Alex and Joey aren't doing anything to attract attention to themselves in the parking lot or we'll end up being made.

The inside is just as busy as the outside. I take my place in line, and after a couple minutes, it's my turn to step up to the counter. "Reservation for Monroe," I tell the clerk. I leave out my first name, trying not to say it out loud if possible. Fortunately for me, the girl working the counter either isn't a fan, is too busy to notice, or is extremely discrete, because she doesn't bat an eye as she pulls up the reservation.

"We've got you down for six adults and one child for a horse tour at eleven. Is your entire party here?" Despite the frenzied atmosphere, the clerk is cool, calm and collected.

"Yes, they're all outside."

"Great. All the adults will need to sign a waiver, and the child's parent or guardian can include the child on their form. We do it all electronically, so if you can get everyone to come inside to take care of that, you'll be all set."

I nod, knowing I'll have to send them in one-by-one or two-by-two for minimal impact. We're easier to spot as a group.

"Oh, and sir, we are running just a little behind schedule this morning," she smiles apologetically. "One of our drivers called out. But by the time we get your group signed in and loaded into your vehicle, the replacement driver should be here and ready to take y'all out."

"That sounds fine. I'll let the rest of the group know to come inside and sign the waivers."

She smiles in response and lets me know where we'll load the vehicle. I thank her and head back outside, placing my sunglasses back over my eyes. Fortunately, I don't see Alex or Joey running around the parking lot. Unfortunately, I don't see them at all.

"Where are Tweedle Dee and Tweedle Dum?" I ask Chase, who is leaning on the outside of the van.

He nods his head towards the gated section of the parking lot. I look over and see Alex and Joey engaged in a very animated conversation with a long-haired, surfer-looking dude. He's walking them to different ATVs, probably explaining the specs for the different models.

"We need to sign waivers. Why don't you and Ally go on in, I'll send Evie in behind you and round up the other two." I don't need to explain the spacing to Chase. He knows as well as I do that it's best for us to split up in public. He gets Ally out of the car and lets Evie know that she and Max are up next. I walk over to where Joey and Alex are.

"This one here is a five-speed, best we've got."

"Dude, it's a Raptor," Alex says excitedly, nudging Joey in the arm.

As the guy sees me approach, his smile widens along with his eyes, and I know we've been made. Apparently Sand Tours really does pride themselves on their discretion because he doesn't say a word.

"Hey, we've all got to sign waivers inside," I tell Joey and Alex. "Give the girls a minute to get through. When you're done, meet us on the other side to load up."

Alex and Joey nod, and their attention goes right back to surfer dude. I listen to his spiel for a little bit since I actually am interested in an ATV rental at some point on this trip, then thank surfer dude, who introduces himself as Karl, for his time, and nudge the guys along when I see Evie exit the building.

Joey and Alex walk inside, and I walk around to the side of the building where I was told we'll be loading up. I see Ally, Evie, and Max standing on the sidewalk beside a large four-wheel drive pick-up truck with the Sand Tours logo on the side. There are three bucket seats lined up on either side of the truck bed, and a roof on top with open sides. Chase is in the bed of the truck, buckling in Max's car seat.

"One of us is gonna have to sit up front," Ally says once I'm standing with them.

I knew this from when I made the reservation. "Yeah, I'll do it. I don't mind."

Ally furrows her brow, "I don't want you to miss out, Trev."

"I won't miss out. I'll probably have a better view than all of you." She studies me, trying to see if I really don't mind, or if I'm doing my usual and taking one for the team so my siblings and friends can have a good time. The truth is, I'm doing both. "Look, if it makes you feel better...if we have fun and decide to do it again, someone else can sit in the front next time."

Ally smiles, "Yeah, okay." She and Evie hop up in the bed and sit on either side of Max's car seat. I boost Max over the side—which he gets an absolute kick out of—and Evie buckles him in. Chase hops in opposite Ally, and I lean against the truck bed, waiting on Joey, Alex, and our driver.

Just as Alex and Joey step out of the building, a muddy Jeep Wrangler comes rushing into the lot and jerks into a parking space, barking its tires. Muttered curse words in the most angelic of tones float across the parking lot, and I couldn't tear my eyes, or ears, away from the spectacle if I tried.

The most beautiful woman I've ever seen gets out of said Jeep, slams the door, and kicks it for good measure. She tips her head back and closes her eyes, her full lips moving though I can't hear what she's saying. I wish I could hear what she was saying.

I take a moment to completely check her out: long, tan legs, denim short-shorts, white tank top with pink bikini straps peeking out around her neck. She's barefoot, and something about that is sexy as hell. Her long, brown hair is in a thick braid down her back.

"Holy hot chick," Alex says, not quietly, beside me.

Holy Hot Chick straightens herself out; her eyes zero in on our group—all staring in wonder now. She's probably wondering who called her "hot chick," then after staring at us—at me—for a good thirty seconds, she huffs and storms into the building.

"Bitches be crazy," Alex says with a shrug, then hops in the back and begins arguing with Joey about who gets to sit across from Max. "Sit across from your wife...Max wants to sit across from his favorite uncle. Don't ya buddy?"

"Unca! Unca!"

"Told you!" Alex laughs victoriously. I shake my head; the antics never seem to end.

The side door of the building pops open and the beautiful brunette from the Jeep appears. Smiling and confident, she walks right up to me—her bare feet now covered in flip-flops that are smacking against the pavement—and sticks her hand out.

"You must be Mr. Monroe. I'm Sara, I'll be your driver today."

I'm not entirely sure, but I think my jaw drops for a second before I take her hand and shake. What I'd really like to do is bring her hand up to my lips and kiss it like the goddess I'm positive she must be.

"Trevor. Please, call me Trevor. Mr. Monroe was my dad." I smile, slightly stumbling over my words.

"This is gonna be epic," I hear Alex say in a stage whisper behind me. Sad thing is, he probably thought he was actually whispering.

"Sorry about him," I say, still shaking her hand. *Why am I still holding her hand?* "Sorry," I grimace, quickly letting go.

"It's okay," she smiles. "I guess you're riding with me?" she asks, raising her brow and drawing my attention from her mouth to the most amazing blue eyes I've ever seen.

"Yeah, I'm riding you. *With* you. I'm riding *with* you. Shit." I tip my head back and close my eyes, very similar to her posture from a few minutes ago. "I'm sorry," I say, but I'm not sure she can hear me over Alex and

Joey's uproarious laughter from the back of the truck. I finally open my eyes and chance a look at her and see that she's laughing a little, too.

"You'll have to take me to dinner first," she winks. "As for the tour, why don't you get in the front seat while I check to make sure everyone's seat belts are secure?"

"Can you secure my seat belt for me?" Alex asks. "Ow, what the hel—heck did you do that for?" Alex glares at Ally.

"Behave yourself!" she growls.

"Chase, control your woman! Ow! Son of a—! Switch with me Joe, sit across from your kid. Come on."

"You think my wife won't kick you?"

"Trev, I'll sit up front," Alex says, making a move to rise.

"Sorry," Sara says, patting Alex on the shoulder. "Trevor's too tall to sit back here. It's in the rule book."

"But I was born a rule breaker, baby." Alex says, waggling his eyebrows and giving his best grin.

"You were not," Ally interjects. "If anyone was born a rule breaker, it was me."

"You were slow. That hardly makes you a rule breaker."

"I was supposed to be first."

"And that just means you've been failing to meet expectations since birth. Not that you're a rule breaker."

Ally glares at Alex, then looks at Chase expectantly. He rolls his eyes, but still elbows Alex in the side.

"Ow, what was that for?"

"Stop disrespecting your sister. You're being an ass."

"Language," Evie calls out.

"Sorry," Chase says.

"She started it," Alex complains. "I only said I was born a rule breaker; she's the one who started arguing with me."

"Are they always like this?" Sara asks me as we both take a seat in the cab.

"Yes. At least once a day, every day."

"Brother and sister?" she asks.

"Twins." I answer as I buckle my seat belt.

Her eyes dart up to mine with genuine interest, "Really?"

"Yep."

"That's so cool. My niece and nephew are fraternal twins." She smiles that heart-stopping smile again, and I swear my ability to form a sentence goes straight out the window. "Ever since they were born I've been intrigued by research on twins and twin studies. Interesting stuff."

"Well, you don't want to research these twins. Trust me."

She laughs, and if her smile hadn't already knocked me on my ass, her laugh would have. It was ethereal; it suited her other angelic qualities...like her voice and her eyes and her smile...

"I sense there is a definite warning there," she says, still laughing.

"Yes. It says 'Proceed with Caution.'"

"You're funny, Trevor Monroe." I love the way my full name rolls off her tongue. Sara puts the key in the ignition and turns on the truck. The rumble of the engine cuts off conversation in the back. She grabs a small, black, wireless device from the dash and clips it to the strap of her tank top. I'm completely mesmerized by her simple movements.

Sara taps the roof of the truck through her open window, pops it into gear, and we're off. She presses a button on the steering wheel and a red light blinks on the wireless device. When she speaks, her voice comes through the speakers.

"Hey everyone, thanks for choosing Sand Tours. I'm Sara Sands, and I'll be your guide today."

Chapter Four

Sara

This is shaping up to be one of the worst days of the year.

First, my Jeep ends up stuck in the mud in the driveway—mud caused by my older, yet clearly not more mature, sister throwing a hissy fit last night and having her man of the hour do donuts outside the house. After it had rained all day. I lost my damn show in that mud...I liked that sandal.

If I wasn't half asleep, I would have been able to easily avoid getting stuck. I mean I drive four-by-fours on the beach, surely I can get through some mud.

But no. Not this morning.

Why? Because my coffee machine broke. I cannot function without my caffeine. And I really can't function without caffeine on too few hours of sleep. Which is what happened last night because Gwen, my niece, kept having nightmares and couldn't sleep. I wasn't at all surprised given the out-of-nowhere and damn near violent visit from her mother. My sister is a real class act. Mother of the year, for sure.

The positive taken from the mud incident? My niece and nephew were entertained to the max, and it really brightened their spirits after last night's debacle.

I was late dropping them off to day camp and subsequently late for my quarterly meeting with my accountant, which, of course, didn't last more than fifteen minutes before I was interrupted by Victoria at the shop telling me that Paul had called out—again—and we had no other driver available for the eleven o'clock private tour. I'd tried to get her to just reschedule the tour, but she told me this group had scheduled several different tours and rentals over the next few weeks, and she was afraid rescheduling the first event may cause them to cancel the rest. Very valid concern, which is exactly why she runs the front of the shop.

So I apologized profusely to my accountant—for the lack of shoes, thank goodness we live in a beach town, and for cancelling the meeting—and hit the road.

Where I got a flat tire.

I'm not even making this up. This is my life today!

Fortunately I keep a can of that flat tire foam stuff in the Jeep in case of emergency, and since I didn't have the kids in the car, and I was only a mile or so from the shop, I attached the nozzle to the tire and let it do its thing, making a quick call to Victoria with my ETA. She informed me the private group had just arrived.

Great.

When I pulled into the shop's parking lot like a bat outta hell about ten minutes later, I'm lucky I didn't hit any pedestrians. Then I practically fell out of the Jeep since I just couldn't help myself and *had* to get stuck in the seat belt. I kicked the stupid car, even though it's totally not the car's fault— although most of this morning's calamities have involved it. Something I can stew about later.

I tipped my head back, closed my eyes, and prayed to all that is holy that this private group isn't full of rude snobs, screaming children, shriekers, gigglers, or anything else that falls into the obnoxious category.

Who am I kidding? *Everyone* falls into that category today.

I'm broken from my perfect little moment by a male voice saying, "holy hot chick." I snap my head down and look in the direction of the voice. Standing by the truck, the truck

I'll be taking out in just a few short minutes, are two of the most beautiful men I've ever seen.

They look so much alike, they have to be related. The taller, more handsome one looks a little bit older. His hair is a slightly darker shade than the shorter one. The shorter one has a shit-eating grin on his face, and I immediately know he's the one with the big mouth. He's gorgeous, but the tall one? I can't take my eyes off him. And he can't seem to take his eyes off of me, either.

Shit!

Now he clearly knows I'm staring at him. At least he was staring at me, too. I can use that in a court of law. Frustrated with myself for wasting even more time, I exhale, rather dramatically I might add, and stalk off towards the front door to the shop. I usually use the employee entrance on the side, but I need a minute to compose myself before getting that close to Mr. Beautiful and the rest of his beautiful people.

"Thank God you're here!" Victoria calls out as soon as I open the door.

"I told you I was coming. Of course I'm here," I snap, hurrying to the locker room to grab a pair of flip-flops from my locker.

Victoria takes a step back, obviously shocked at my tone. "Right, well, the private group is already set up with their vehicle. They should be loading up as we speak."

"Thanks, Vic. I'm sorry. I just had a horrible night, and a worse morning. If that's even possible. Good call on calling me in," I tell her as I look up the group in the computer. They have twelve additional bookings over the next four weeks. "Would have sucked to lose all this."

"Not to mention, they're not at all hard to look at," she winks, and I blush. "Oh so you saw them, huh? Wonder what their story is...why they wanted a private tour and all that."

I shrug my shoulders. "Not my business." I grab a bottled water from the fridge behind the desk and give Victoria a quick salute. "See ya later!"

Walking to the side door, I give myself a pep talk. *I can do this. I'm a professional. It doesn't matter if the guy is gorgeous. I've seen other gorgeous men before. I've given beautiful people tours before, even. This will be a piece of cake!* I school my expression: cool, calm, collected, confident. Paste on smile. Open door. *Let's do this!*

I walk right up to Mr. Beautiful and introduce myself, pretending he didn't see me in all my glory at my Jeep just a few minutes earlier. He stumbles over his words a bit, clearly as affected by me as I am by him. This pleases me, and I smile wider, but it's useless.

He's on vacation. I live here. End of story.

Laughter from the truck bed breaks our little moment, and as I excuse myself to do a safety check, the one who I decide is Trevor's brother, the one with the mouth, asks me to help him with his seat belt. This begins a verbal sparring match between him and a pretty girl with the same sandy blonde hair. This must be his sister. They bicker like only siblings can.

"Are they always like this?" I ask Trevor once he and I are seated in the cab.

"Yes. At least once a day. Every day," he responds.

"Brother and sister?" I ask, already knowing the answer.

"Twins."

"Really?" I look at him to see if he's joking, then glance in the rear view mirror at the two of them. You can definitely tell they are siblings just by looking at them, that's for sure. Same hair and eyes. Even their skin tone is similar. Obviously they aren't identical, but they have similar facial features as well.

"Yep," Trevor answers.

"That's so cool. My niece and nephew are fraternal twins. Ever since they were born I've been intrigued by research on twins and twin studies. Interesting stuff." I trail off when I realize I'm babbling. Trevor grew up with twins, I'm sure he knows all about this stuff and probably doesn't care to get my take on it. I smile and go about my pre-tour checklist in my head.

"Well, you don't want to research these twins. Trust me," he says, but you can hear the emotion in his voice. He loves his siblings, that much is clear.

I laugh and say, "I sense there is a definite warning there."

"Yes. It says 'Proceed with Caution.'"

I laugh some more. "You're funny Trevor Monroe."

I start the truck and grab the wireless mic off the dash, attaching it to my tank top. My movements are a little jerky, nervous, as I'm all too aware of Trevor's gaze on me. I can feel it like a caress, watching my every movement.

I do my usual double-tap on the roof, letting any staff in the vicinity know we're heading out, then put the truck in drive and pull away from the curb. Once we're out of the parking lot and on the main road, I press the button on the steering wheel so that my voice comes through the sound system.

"Hey, everyone, thanks for choosing Sand Tours. I'm Sara Sands, and I'll be your guide today." Out of the corner of my eye I see Trevor's eyes widen at my last name, and I can sense his wheels are turning. He's asking himself whether or not it's a coincidence. Perhaps a stage name?

Nope, I silently answer, *can't say it is*. Although I guess it kind of is a coincidence that my last name is 'Sands' and I live on the beach and do beach tours. But whatever. Truth is, I own Sand Tours, built it from the ground up with my then boyfriend who I bought out just over two years ago.

Sand Tours is my baby. Always has been. Always will be. Aside from my niece and nephew, it's the only thing I have time for in my life, and I certainly won't let a passerby interfere with that. Not even one as beautiful as Trevor Monroe.

Chapter Five

Trevor

Sara Sands.

A beautiful name for a beautiful woman.

I wonder if the last name has as much to do with the company as it suggests. She *could* be a business owner. I haven't spoken more than one hundred words to her, but she seems smart and confident enough to run her own shop. Maybe it's a family thing.

She proceeds to inform us about today's excursion. Tells us how much more road we'll ride on before we hit the beach. She explains the terrain, and what to expect when we're riding on the sand.

Alex and Joey are whooping and hollering in the back, clearly looking forward to this adventure. Max is eating up his father and uncle's antics. Chase, Ally, Evie, and I are taking it all in stride, like we always do.

Sara uses the time on the paved road to tell us about the history of the herds of wild horses on the northern part of the Outer Banks. She knows a lot about the Spanish Mustangs, how they arrived, and their current numbers. I'm surprised when she tells us there are less than one hundred.

"From what you said earlier, it sounds like we've covering a pretty expansive area. Won't it be like trying to find a needle in a haystack with less than one hundred horses to look for?" Evie asks Sara and damned if I'm not hanging on in anticipation for her response.

"Good question," Sara starts. "You're right in that the area isn't exactly overflowing with horses. It makes them pretty hard to find if they're not out in the open, unless you know where to look for them. And today is your lucky day because I happen to know where they like to hang out."

She smiles that breathtaking smile and winks at me...suddenly I don't care about the horses. I just want to spend time with her. Alone. Not trapped in a tin can with my family.

You're on a family *vacation, Trevor,* I remind myself. 'Family' *being the key word.*

I love my family, don't get me wrong. Anyone who has met me knows I love my family. I would do anything for them. I *have* done everything for them. But right now, right this instant...I want to be selfish and do something for me. I want to think only of myself. I want to throw them out of the truck and drive away with Sara.

"Horsies Momma! See horsies!" Max cries out.

"Yes, baby," Evie smiles. "We're gonna see horsies."

Sara beams in the rear view mirror. She clearly has a soft spot for kids. "How old is he?" she asks me.

Her mic is off and the only sound is the wind whipping around the cab through the open windows.

"Three."

"He's precious. He belongs to the pixie and the beard?" she asks, and I laugh at her description of Evie and Joey. It's quite perfect.

"Yes. Evie, the pixie, is his mom, and Joey, the beard, is his dad."

She gives a sheepish smile and shrugs her shoulders. "Some days I meet so many people, I just don't even bother trying to overhear and remember names."

"I know exactly what you mean," I tell her as I relax back into my seat. And I do know exactly what she means. On tour, it's hard enough remembering the names of the other bands' crews, let alone the crews at the different venues, the fans, media personalities...the list is endless.

"Oh, yeah? Do you give tours when you're not on vacation?" she jokes.

She has no idea just how close to being right she is. I consider telling her the truth about who I am, who *we* are, but I don't think I can do it. Having her treat me like a person, not a star, has been wonderful. None of us expect to make it through this trip without being outed at some point, but it seems a bit counterproductive to out myself.

But...I don't think I can lie to her. And a lie of omission is still a lie.

Shit. What am I even talking about? She's our tour guide, for crying out loud. She could be married for all I know, even though she isn't wearing a ring—yeah, I checked. Regardless, I shouldn't be concerned with sharing my identity or lying to her. I'll probably never see her again after today. That last thought causes an ache deep down in my chest, and I'm not quite sure what to do about it.

"Trevor, you okay?" Sara asks, her eyes wide and alert.

That's when I realize I'm rubbing the emotional ache in my chest. I straighten up in my seat and smile at her.

"Sorry, heartburn," I lie. *Stupid.*

"You sure you're okay?" She's still looking at me with concern.

"Yeah," I nod. "I'm fine."

"Okay. Good. So tell me about this crazy bunch you've got here with you." She nods her head toward the truck bed where the crazy bunch is.

"You sure you want to know?" I laugh.

Do I tell her? Don't I tell her?

"Of course! I spend most of my time now in the office and shop; I don't get to meet people the way I used to when I did the tours."

"You run this place?" I ask, hoping to deter her line of questioning.

"Yep, it's my pride and joy."

"It's amazing." *You're amazing.* "Y'all offer so much. People must love you to allow for such expansion."

She nods. "We started out really small, my former partner and I, and every now and then we added something new, and it just grew like a weed. A good friend of mine is my Assistant Manager. She's been with me from the beginning."

I nod, "She's your business partner?"

Sara stiffens slightly and shakes her head. "No. I don't have a partner anymore. I bought him out a couple years ago."

I'm not an idiot, I can pretty much guess what happened there...with *him*. I can tell she's uncomfortable, so I compliment her on her accomplishments. "Well, you've done a great job. The place is amazing and business seems to be booming."

She beams at me, genuinely appreciative of the praise.

"Thanks, Trevor. I love what I do, and I'm so lucky to be as successful as I am. It's all just way beyond my wildest dreams."

"I know exactly what you mean."

She looks at me, tilts her head and raises her eyebrow very quickly before putting her eyes back on the road. "That's the second time you've said that, yet you won't elaborate. Care to share with the rest of the class?"

We're interrupted by Ally tapping on the divider, I sigh in relief. Sara notices and shoots me a strange look.

"What's up?" she calls to the back, flipping on her mic so everyone can hear her.

"What happens if it rains?" Ally asks, gesturing to the dark clouds in the distance.

"We get wet, of course," Sara replies with an easy smile. "Well, Trevor and I not so much because we can roll up the windows.

Y'all on the other hand? You're gonna get soaked!"

We all laugh because it's obvious she's joking around.

"Seriously though, the weather is very unpredictable. It looks ominous now, but by the time we get over there, it may have passed or dissolved. If it's a sprinkle, we'll be okay. If it's heavy or if y'all are uncomfortable at all, we'll head back. Essentially, since this is a private tour, it's *your* tour, so we can do whatever you want as long as it isn't against the rules or the law."

Everyone nods, satisfied with this response. We're not afraid of a little rain.

"Rain sawn! Unca! Rain sawn!"

"Aw, come on kid." Alex whines playfully.

"Pwease! Unca, pwease!" Max sticks out his bottom lip and his eyes are big and wide. He has the puppy dog face perfected.

"What's he asking for?" Sara asks quietly, her mic is back off.

"He wants Alex to sing him the rain song."

She nods like it's the most natural thing in the world. Boy is she in for a treat if he actually starts singing.

Chapter Six

Sara

"Hum it out for me, Chase." The brother, now known as Alex, says before clearing his throat.

The quiet one I assume is Chase begins to hum, but instead of the childlike "Rain, Rain Go Away" I expected to hear, he's humming something soft and low. It sounds familiar, but I can't quite make it out over the rumble of the engine and the wind.

I'm momentarily stunned when Alex opens his mouth and starts to sing. He has an amazing voice. And he's singing...he's singing Breaking Benjamin? I chuckle to myself when I realize the "rain song" this three-year-old just asked for was "Rain" by Breaking Benjamin.

Alex is taking some liberties with the lyrics to make it more appropriate for a three-year-old, and Max is eating it up, just loving every minute of it. Jeez, if I had an uncle with that voice, I'd be asking him to sing to me all the time, too. And Chase, the one humming, he's so in tune. They're amazing together. They've got to be musicians.

Alex can sing. Chase can hum. Yeah...so that's not exactly an instrument. I look in the rear view mirror and catch the bearded one, I think his name was Joey, tapping his hands on his knees, seemingly in tune. Drummer? Out of the corner of my eye I check out Trevor. He's not making any movements, but I see his hands look a little rough and callused. Maybe he plays the guitar?

"What's on your mind?" Trevor asks, rolling his head to the left to look at me.

"Your brother has a great voice," I say, hoping he'll add to it. I didn't miss how he dodged my questions earlier. He's hiding something. Not that he has to share anything with me. I'm just the tour guide.

"He does," he nods.

So that's how he wants to play it. Okay. "And Chase sure can hum," I say. Maybe with a little more attitude than I'd intended judging by how quickly his head snaps in my direction.

"Uh, yeah. He plays the guitar."

Hm, so I was wrong about Trevor. Chase is the guitar player. "Are they in a band or something?"

Trevor sighs. "Can you keep a secret?" I nod enthusiastically, knowing that I've got him, and he laughs. "Joey, Alex, Chase and I are in a band. It's pretty popular, and we've got a little break now so we're taking a vacation. Ally, my sister, just graduated college so we could all finally take time off together. It's long overdue. Anyway, we are trying to stay on the down low. We know we'll probably get recognized at some point, but we're doing our best to stay as inconspicuous as possible."

I nod in understanding. That makes sense. Being on the road and in the spotlight is probably exhausting.

"What's the name of your band?"

"JACT," he says, and my heart stops.

"JACT?" I repeat.

"Yeah. Why? Have you heard of us?"

Have I heard of them? What a *stupid* question! Who hasn't heard of them? I don't watch much TV besides children's programs, and I sure as hell don't get to go to concerts, so I'm not sure I've ever seen the faces that belong to the sounds of one of the greatest rock bands I've ever heard. I immediately replay Alex singing "Rain" in my head, how did I not recognize his voice?

"So you *have* heard of us..." Trevor says, chuckling at my deer-caught-in-the-headlights look.

"Uh, duh," I say, rather eloquently, I might add.

"I take it you're a fan?"

"Yeah. You guys are awesome. I admit you're not my *favorite* band..." *Did I really just say that?* "But you are definitely one of the best groups I've heard in a long time. I knew something was up when Alex sang that song. *That* kind of talent isn't normal. But don't worry, your secret is safe with me." I take in a big breath after blowing out all that word vomit.

Trevor laughs. "Good to know."

"So that's what all the privacy was about, huh?"

"Yeah, we really just needed a break from reality, you know?" *Do I ever...* "It was lucky that we could all take the time off together. Ally and Chase just got engaged, so we're kind of celebrating that, too. Trying to give them some time to themselves before the vipers get ahold of the story and run with it. I try to keep my sister out of the spotlight as much as possible. I want her to have a normal life."

"Is it really that tough being a celebrity?" I ask. "I don't mean that in a bad way," I quickly amend, realizing how that probably came off. "It's just that I read about the lifestyle being very exposed and people being very intrusive and mean, and I guess I'm just wondering if all that is real."

Trevor sighs. "It is and it isn't."

"Hold that thought," I interrupt and press the button to activate the mic. "Folks, we're about to hit Ocean Highway so things are going to get a little bumpy. Keep your arms, legs, and ears inside the vehicle. Keep your safety belts secure and hang on. If things get too rough or you need me to slow down, just give me a shout. Otherwise I'm going to keep a pretty steady pace. If you stop or go too slow in the sand, you're more likely to get stuck. That's not saying you can't go slow or you can't stop, just that it'll take a little extra umph to get going again and we don't like to stress our engines too much. Anyone have any questions?"

"Horsies!" Adorable little Max calls from the back, and we all laugh.

"Real soon, buddy. We have to drive down the beach for a little bit to get to where the horsies are, first."

He nods as though he understands me completely, and I smile as his mother brushes one of his dark curls off his forehead.

"You have a lovely family," I tell Trevor after I turn the mic off.

"They're the best," he agrees.

"So where were we? Oh! Celebrity-dom. Is that even a term?" I laugh.

"Not sure. You should copyright it, just in case." He grins at me, then winks, and I feel a burst of warmth from somewhere inside of me...somewhere that's been dormant a while.

"I might just do that," I wink back.

I can't believe I'm flirting with him! He's not just some hot guy now, he's a famous hot guy. And I realize, sadly, that thoughts like that are exactly what he seems to want to avoid on this trip. He just wants to be a regular guy for the summer. Understandably so.

"You don't have to talk about it," I quickly say, the guilt setting in.

He looks over to me, surprise evident on his face. "I don't mind."

"Nah, this kind of thing is what you're trying to avoid, right? And here I am prying into your personal life."

"You're not prying. We're just two people talking about our day jobs."

I laugh at his simplification of the situation. "I suppose so."

"We—the band—pretty much keep our lives low key. We don't do everything to the nines like some Hollywood celebs do. And that has its positives and its negatives. On the one hand, it kind of gives off an elusive vibe, so that when people catch sight of us, they jump for a chance at a photo or story. On the other hand, it lets us live a relatively calm life outside of touring and appearances."

"That doesn't sound too bad."

"It's not. But it's why Chase and Ally's engagement getting out would spin our world on its axis."

"Like living under a microscope."

"It could be," he nods.

"What about the rest of your family? Your parents? Any other siblings?"

Trevor's face goes dark for a moment before he says, "This is it. We're all each other has."

Chapter Seven

Trevor

Sara goes quiet, and I instantly feel bad. My statement—not the words so much as my tone—sort of killed the buzz we had going between us.

"I'm sorry," I say honestly.

She looks at me oddly. "You're sorry? No, I'm sorry. If there is one thing I'm good at, it's sticking my foot in my mouth."

"You didn't stick your foot in your mouth."

"I did. I should have realized if you wanted me to know you would have told me. You've been very forthcoming and I, of all people, should know better than to pry about family."

I wonder what she means by that...but just like she said, I know better than to pry about family. But I sure wish she'd tell me.

"Sara, it's okay."

She stops shaking her head and glances at me, giving me a quick smile. "You're really sweet, Trevor." Her eyes widen a little, as if she surprised herself by saying that, and I catch her cheeks pink before she turns to face the road again. Or the beach rather.

I've been so consumed with our conversation—with Sara—that I've barely registered the rough ride and gorgeous scenery. On the right is the ocean...as in it's *right* there, maybe twenty feet away. On the left are small sand dunes, and beyond those are large beach homes. Straight ahead are other vehicles. Some heading in the same direction as us, others passing by in the opposite direction. It truly is an ocean highway.

"Pretty amazing, isn't it?" her soft voice says.

"I've never seen anything like it." She laughs, a musical sound, at the awe in my voice. "This is so cool. I bet a lot of people get stuck though."

"Yeah, there's always at least one when I'm out here."

"You said you don't do tours much anymore, does that mean you drive out here for fun?" I really want to know more about her. Ideally, I'd like to know everything about her, but this short tour won't allow for that.

"Yeah, I love the beach. I take my niece and nephew out here as often as I can." That's the second time she's mentioned her niece and nephew. They must be close to her.

I'm about to ask about them when she slows the vehicle and starts talking into the mic.

"Okay guys, we're going to make a left here and head up over that dune. I can't use the mic on that side of the hill so you'll have to get used to me yelling. I'm going to take us to a spot where one of the guides reported seeing a group of horses just this morning. Doesn't necessarily mean anything, since they move around quite a bit, but it's nice and shady over there so we might get lucky."

Max squeals from the back, excited about the prospect of finally seeing some horses and begins asking Sara a ton of questions, which Evie translates. Sara patiently answers each and every one of them, making it clear that she's got experience with kids. Whether it's from her niece and nephew or from doing tours, she's a pro.

Sara's and my conversation is placed on the backburner as we drive through the sand trails behind the dunes. She animatedly tells us stories about the land, the wildlife, and the homes as we go. I can tell she loves what she does, and she loves this place. It's the same passion I see in myself when I talk about and play my music.

I sit back and take in the smell of the sea, the whip of the wind and dust on my face, and the heat from the sun. I'm sure I'm going to have a nice lopsided burn on my right side by the time the tour is over. But I can think of worse ways to spend my day. If it wasn't for Sara's musical voice and angelic laughter, the sounds of the waves crashing on the shore and the occasional caw of a sea bird could lull me to sleep.

But I don't want to miss a thing—not a moment of this time spent with her. No matter how insignificant it may seem.

"MOMMA! HORSIES!" Max screams from the back of the truck, and we all jerk our heads around to find it.

Sure enough, on the top of a nearby hill, there are a couple of dark brown horses. Sara drives by real slow, letting us know that she can't stop the vehicle on these trails, but she's still trying to give us an opportunity to see the animals and take pictures.

The rest of the morning is much of the same. Max has hawk eyes and seems to spot the horses before anyone else, and he lets everyone within a mile radius know all about it with his squeals. Evie takes a ton of pictures, and we're all smiling and laughing the entire ride. By the time we're on the paved road headed back to the shop, Max has been lulled to sleep by the wavy motion of the

Ocean Highway, and a peaceful calm has settled in around us. I think Joey and Alex are even asleep. Life on a tour bus will do that to you—you can practically fall asleep standing up.

We return to the parking lot and Sara pulls up on the side of the building where we loaded up just two hours ago. Two hours flashed by in the blink of an eye and now I have to say goodbye to her with no good, unselfish reason to see her again. Sure we can schedule another tour, and we have some scheduled out in the future with Sand Tours, but there's no guarantee she'll be part of those.

I get out of the cab when Sara does and walk around to the back to help the girls get down. When Ally hops down, she wraps her arms around my neck and hugs me.

"That was so much fun, big brother."

I smile down at her, "Yeah it was, kid."

She scrunches up her nose and pinches my cheek at the endearment, then laughs and bounces off to Chase's side, grabs hold of his hand, and leans her head on his shoulder. I smile as I look around at the group; everyone is the picture of contentment. Well, everyone except Alex who is staring at the mom-mobile like it contains the plague.

"So what do you think?" I hear Ally say to Sara.

"Oh...I don't know," Sara answers, glancing at me briefly and then looking down at the ground.

I step over to where Sara, Ally, and Evie stand. "What's going on?"

"We're going to grill tonight," Ally tells me. "We invited Sara to join us."

Have I mentioned how much I love my sister?

"That's a great idea," I agree, looking at Sara.

She looks up at me and smiles shyly. "I'd love to, but I've got my niece and nephew tonight-"

"Bring them," Evie interrupts. "We've got the pool and Max loves hanging out with other kids. I was worried that he wouldn't get to spend time with any kids on this trip— aside from his father and uncle."

She seems to fight an inner battle for a minute, twisting her hands in front of her, before she finally nods. "Yeah, okay. I guess it will be okay."

"Great," Ally smiles and claps. "We'll write down the address for you. It's in Duck." Ally and Evie head over to the van, I assume Ally is looking for a pen and some paper and Evie is probably looking to get Max loaded up since Joey has secured the car seat.

Sara looks up at me, and I smile. "I'm glad you're coming over."

"You are?" her eyebrows lift in surprise.

"Yeah. I enjoyed talking with you today. I'd like to be able to talk to you more."

She blushes and looks down again, not at all the uber-confident woman I met in this same spot a couple hours ago. "I liked talking to you, too."

My answering grin stretches clear across my face but before I can say anything, Ally is back and handing Sara a piece of paper.

"Can you do six?" Ally asks.

"That should be fine. We have the second shift coming in to do tours this afternoon, so as long as none of them call out, I'll be free."

"Great," Ally smiles. "We'll see you later then. Come on, big brother. Alex is gonna flip his lid if he has to spend any more time than necessary in the van." She loops her arm in mine and starts tugging me away.

I look over my shoulder at Sara. "See you later, Sara," I call.

"Bye, Trevor." She watches us walk away for a second, then shakes her head and goes into the door of the shop.

"Smooth, big brother. Real smooth. You need to work on your game." Ally laughs as we approach the van.

I look at her in shock. "What are you talking about?" Was my attraction to Sara really that obvious?

"Oh don't play dumb," she says once we're seated inside. This is NOT a conversation I feel like having in front of the entire group. But ever since Ally and Chase's blow up, very few secrets are kept anymore. "You've got it bad for Sara!" Ally teases and everyone laughs.

"I do not," I grumble like the petulant twenty-seven year old that I am.

"Right," Alex scoffs from the passenger seat. "You were tripping all over your words earlier. *'Oh Sara, I wanna ride you.'*"

"I did not say that!" I pop Alex in the arm.

"Actually, you kind of did," Chase inserts, and I glare at him in the rear view mirror. Some best friend. "Minus the 'oh Sara' part, of course."

"Whatever."

"You're welcome, big brother!" Ally winks from the middle row.

This is going to be an interesting night.

Chapter Eight

Sara

I can't believe I agreed to go to their house for dinner tonight. What was I thinking? Dark blue eyes and a killer smile flash through my mind. Yep, that's what I was thinking alright.

I'm sitting alone in the Jeep with my head lying on the steering wheel, face tilted towards the house. The twins flew from the vehicle the moment we stopped in the driveway, they are currently chasing each other around the wraparound porch. Or rather Georgie appears to be chasing Gwen. He's probably holding a bug or something. Boys can be so gross, there's just no telling.

Sighing, I get out of the Jeep and trudge up the wooden stairs to the front door. The kids come around the corner, and Gwen tries to hide behind me as Georgie dances around us with a worm dangling from his hand. Six-year-old boys are awesome. Just awesome.

"Georgie, stop teasing your sister. Gwen, if you keep running around me and bumping into me, I'll never make it in the house, and we've got to hustle or we're going to be late." It's already a quarter after five, and it's going to take a good twenty to thirty minutes to get to the Monroes' house with the dinner traffic. I love where I live, and it's obviously conducive for business, but summer tourist traffic is a bear.

They finally quit fooling around, and Georgie chucks the worm off the side of the deck. Thank God! I enjoy fishing as much as any islander, but worms are just disgusting. I shiver at the thought alone.

"Where are we going?" Gwen asks once I unlock the door and we all pour inside.

"We were asked to go to dinner by some new friends. They have a little boy; he's three. And they have a pool."

Gwen's eyes light up when I mention Max; she loves kids—no matter the age. She's my little nurturer. Georgie, on the other hand, his eyes light up when I mention the pool. The kid is like a fish, and while my home may be on the beach, we don't have a pool, so the kid gets a lot less water time than one might think. Can't just let six year olds out in the ocean in any conditions. I've taught them both not to fear the water, but to respect it.

"Awesome!" they both shout, little fists pumping in the air. They take off up the stairs for their rooms, I imagine to get their swimsuits on.

I set my keys on the entry table and hang my bag on the hook. Taking a quick look around, I realize that my house is an absolute pigsty, and with the way things have been at work lately, it's going to stay that way. I had a decent crew at the beginning of the summer, but two of my best guides unexpectedly quit—for legitimate reasons, though—so I desperately hired a couple replacements, and they aren't quite working out.

Sighing, I glance around the messy house. Unlike many of the vacation homes on the coast, the entire first floor of my home is the living space. It's an open floor plan with a large family room, spacious kitchen and a formal dining room turned playroom for the twins. There are four bedrooms upstairs, and the twins love that they have their own rooms. When my sister isn't on a bender, there is even a room up there for her, not that she's ever used it.

While I wait for the kids to get ready, I pick up some of the larger toys laying around and appropriately deposit them into the blue or pink toy chests in the playroom. The twins have been living with me for the past four years. When they were two years old, and I was just twenty-one, my older sister by six years, Nora, got herself arrested for possession of narcotics. I was already keeping the twins under temporary guardianship because they'd been taken away from her due to neglect.

Think that's bad? Well, it gets worse. The guy she was shacking up with at the time was actually manufacturing meth and growing marijuana. She ended up going to prison for possession and distribution, as well as accessory to manufacturing, cultivation, and trafficking. My parents were not fit to raise the twins, and their father is completely out of the picture. Truth is, I don't think my sister knows who their father is. So Auntie Sara became Mommy Sara, though the kids still call me Auntie.

I was twenty-one years old, working on my business degree at the local community college and dating Lucas, my ex-business partner. We had big dreams for Sand Tours, a play on my last name, and kids didn't work into the equation. But I love my niece and nephew, so I did the responsible thing and took them in, not able to imagine them being placed in foster care and possibly separated.

It worked out for a while, Lucas and my dreams came true and Sand Tours was born. We did exceptionally well and business boomed. We even expanded our services when the demand was there. For me, things couldn't be better. Lucas and I were living our dream—or at least I thought we were. I know I was.

I shake off the negative thoughts and head upstairs to get my own swimsuit. Peeking in the twins' rooms as I walk by, I see that they're already in their suits, as I'd suspected, and each settled down with a quiet activity. Georgie is reading and Gwen is brushing her doll's hair. They truly are good kids. I couldn't be more proud of them.

"Five minutes," I call out as I enter my room. I pull out a modest tankini swimsuit; it's sage green and one of my favorites. I have about two drawers full—beach girl here—so that's saying something. I want to look good for Trevor—I'm not going to lie, but I don't want to wear something skimpy around the kids and his family. I quickly wash up in the bathroom and pull on a light green sundress that matches my suit. I wish I had time to shower, but I don't, and I figure it won't hurt since we'll be swimming anyway.

I pull my beach bag out of my closet, tuck the swimsuit inside, and head back downstairs to get some beach towels out of the linen closet. Navy blue for me, pink with seashells for Gwen, and black with bright green monster trucks for Georgie. I holler a last call to the twins and carry my purse and beach bag to the front door. Moments later, I hear the stampede on the hardwood stairs and smile to myself. It all might not be the ideal, but it's my life, and I love it.

Chapter Nine

Trevor

"Jeez, Trev. You're going to wear a hole in the floor," Ally says as I walk by the bay window in the front of the house for the fifteenth time in as many minutes. It's five minutes to six, and Sara should be here any minute. If she comes. I hope she comes.

Damn, I should have gotten her phone number.

"I know what's going through your mind, big brother. She'll be here." Since Ally has gotten her memory back, she's been very intuitive. It's kind of annoying.

"I'm not looking for her." She knows I'm lying. I don't even know why I said it. Ally just smiles and goes back to the kitchen where she and Alex have been prepping the food. Yes, Alex. Turns out he enjoys cooking about as much as his twin and is great at grilling and coming up with tasty marinades and rubs. It's been a great re-bonding experience for the two of them.

I see movement out of the corner of my eye and look out the window. I can't hold back the grin that spreads across my face when I see it's Sara's Jeep. Much to the amusement of my siblings, I eagerly fly down the stairs and to the front door. I pause for a moment, collect myself, then open the door and walk down the steps and across the gravel driveway to the car.

Much to my disappointment, Sara is already out of the car. I would have liked to have opened her door for her. She's got one of the back doors open and is helping the kids out. If she hadn't told me they were her niece and nephew, I would have sworn they were her kids. They look just like her with the same shade of brown hair and blue eyes.

"Hey, guys," I say, squatting down to twins' level. "I'm Trevor, thanks for coming over. What are your names?"

The girl is a little shy, staying back and holding Sara's hand, but the boy steps forward and sticks his hand out to shake mine. "I'm George; that's my twin sister Gwen."

"Nice to meet you, George." I say as I give him a firm shake. "And Gwen," I say, smiling over to her. She gives a shy smile and giggles.

"Everyone calls me Georgie, so you can call me that."

"Sounds like a plan, Georgie." I stand up and meet Sara's eyes. I can't help the smile that spreads across my face. She's so beautiful. "Hi, Sara."

"Hey, Trevor. Thanks again for having us."

"It's no problem. Ally loves to entertain. I'm glad you came," I add, letting her know that I wanted her here, too. I could get lost in her eyes.

"You have a pool?" Georgie asks, reminding me that we aren't alone.

"I do; want to see it?" He nods enthusiastically, and even Gwen seems to perk up. "Well, come on then." I take the lead, and instead of heading up the steps into the house, we walk around the side of the house, past the golf cart that has been supplied for easy beach access, and through the gate into the backyard.

There's little grass back here; it's mostly the concrete pool deck and patio. The pool itself is large and takes up most of the space, then there is a small outdoor kitchen and bar, an area with several lounge chairs, and an outdoor dining table and chairs. Chase,

Alex and Joey are over by the grill, but the girls and Max must still be inside.

Georgie's eyes widen when he sees the pool. "Wow, that's almost as big as the one we go to. Isn't it, Auntie?"

"Yeah, it sure is," Sara agrees.

"When can we swim?" Georgie asks, looking up at me. I look to Sara for guidance.

"After dinner, squirt," she tells him.

"Oh man!" he complains, but you can tell he's not that disappointed. He's too interested in his new surroundings to be upset.

"Hey, little dude," Joey says as he walks over. "We've got a pool table and a foosball table just inside those doors. Wanna play?"

Georgie's eyes widen, and he nods, happily following Joey into the house.

I look at Gwen, who is still hiding behind Sara. "Want to play, too, Gwen?"

She shakes her head 'no' and tucks herself back further.

"Why don't we go inside and see what the girls and Max are up to?" I offer.

Sara nods, and she and Gwen follow me into the house. Georgie is happily twirling the rods of the foosball table, laughing when he gets the ball past Joey's goaltender. Sara smiles at the sight, and I briefly wonder where the twins' parents are.

We take the stairs all the way up to the third floor and find Max sitting on the floor in the living room beating on his toy drums. He's definitely Joey's child. Gwen's eyes widen, and she steps out from behind Sara a little bit, clearly interested in Max.

"That's my nephew, Max," I tell her. "You can go play with him if you'd like."

She looks up at Sara, who nods her approval, and hurries over to the carpet to sit beside Max.

"Hey, Sara," Evie calls out from the kitchen.

"So glad you could make it," Ally adds. "Did you find the house okay?"

"Hi," Sara says, smiling, as she walks up to the kitchen counter. "I had no trouble finding it. I've lived in the area my entire life, so it's not too hard for me to navigate. The hidden drives can be a little tricky, but no trouble tonight."

"Good," Evie says. "The guys already brought the meat out to the grill; we're just finishing up on the salads."

"Can I help with anything?" Sara asks.

"No, we're good. And you're a guest!" Ally admonishes.

"I might be a guest, but you're on vacation."

"Touché," Ally smiles. "But no, thank you. We're almost finished here anyway."

Ally and Evie finish up in the kitchen and walk out to the living room where Max and Gwen are seated, contentedly playing on the rug.

"Who is this beautiful girl?" Evie asks when she sees Gwen.

"Wen," Max says.

"Gwen," Sara says quietly, not wanting Max to get upset at having gotten her name wrong.

"Hello, Gwen," Ally says, squatting down. "My name is Ally, and this is Evie."

Gwen smiles shyly at them, and I'm kind of glad it's not just me she's shy with. I make a silent promise to myself to win this little girl over.

"We're all going to head downstairs now, would you like to help set the table?" Evie asks Gwen. The little girl nods and stands up. Each of the adults grab a dish, and Ally lets Gwen carry the caddy with the plates and silverware. Sara nervously watches Gwen the whole way down the stairs and seems to breathe a sigh of relief when she reaches the bottom without incident.

Joey and Georgie are still at the foosball table, and Sara makes introductions. Georgie is a ham and eats up the attention from the girls.

"How old are you?" Ally asks him.

"Six," he answers, holding up six fingers.

"And how old are you?" she asks Gwen.

"She's six, too," he answers for her.

Ally's eyes widen. "Y'all are twins?" she asks excitedly. They both nod. "I'm a twin, too!"

Georgie and Gwen both brighten up at that. "Really?" Gwen asks quietly, and I'm actually a little jealous my sister got her to speak first. I need to get a grip.

"Yes. My twin brother, Alex, is outside. Come on, let's go meet him!" Abandoning the bowl on the counter, Ally holds out both of her hands and each of the twins take one and walk with her outside.

Sara watches them walk off with a stunned look on her face.

"Ally's just got a way about her," I say.

"Apparently so," she agrees.

Joey picks up Ally's abandoned bowl, and we all tote everything outside to the kitchen, placing the salads in the fridge. A moment later, Ally returns with Gwen and they get to work setting the table.

"I've never seen her take to an adult like that before," Sara confides as we watch Gwen and Ally together.

"There's something about my sister," I tell her. "A kindness, I guess. She just pulls people in."

"I can see that," Sara nods.

I turn towards her and boldly take her hand, "I *am* really glad you came."

She smiles up at me, "Me too."

"Soup's on!" Alex calls, effectively breaking our moment.

"There's something about my brother, too…" I trail off, and she laughs. Still holding her hand, I lead her to the table, making sure she gets a seat right next to me.

Chapter Ten

Sara

Dinner was delicious. We had grilled chicken, steaks, and salmon. With encouragement from Trevor, I sampled a little bit of everything. The twins even tried the salmon, which I have never been able to get them to eat. I'm so stuffed that I have a little food baby happening in my belly and it's not making me want to get in this swimsuit.

I glare at the offending material until there is a knock at the bathroom door. "You okay in there?"

It's Trevor. He's so sweet. Seeing him interact with his family in a natural setting at dinner was incredible. You can tell he is the patriarch of this unconventional family. The way he defuses Ally and Alex's bickering and always seems to have the right answers when any one of them ask about anything. He reminds me a lot of myself.

"Yeah, I'm okay." I reluctantly pull my dress and undergarments off and slip into my bathing suit, thanking myself again for bringing a tankini. I don't have image issues at all, I am very active, so I keep an athletic figure, but I don't think I'm ready for Trevor to see my food baby.

I fold up my clothes in a nice, neat pile, open the door, and step into a wall of muscle.

Trevor is standing in the doorway in a pair of dark blue board shorts. And that's it. I curse his clothing that has hidden his chiseled form from me all day. His chest and arms are tanned and sculpted, like works of art. He's not all beefy and huge...he's just the perfect size.

"Sorry," he says, appearing just as absorbed in my appearance as I am in his. His hands are on my upper arms, holding me upright, and his eyes are taking me in from head to toe and back again, leaving a trail of warmth in their wake.

I've never felt a connection like this before, not even with Lucas, and he was my high school sweetheart; we'd been together for years.

Trevor is staring at my mouth, and I lick my lips. I swear he groans a little.

"We'd better get outside," he says gruffly as he releases me. I instantly miss his touch, but as I hear the squeals of my niece and nephew, I'm quickly reminded that this is not the time, nor the place, to lust over him. In fact, there is no right time or place to do that, really, since his visit here is a temporary one.

I set my clothes down on the counter and follow Trevor outside. I'm not surprised to see Georgie and Gwen splashing around the pool with the other adults. They love the water. I am surprised, however, to see Gwen cheering happily as she's being lifted and thrown into the water by Alex and Joey. She's really opened up to this crew.

I'm not out the door but five seconds before I'm wrapped up in Trevor's strong arms as he jumps into the pool. My head breaks the surface, and I'm sputtering, about ready to rip into him for that, when I hear my niece and nephew's joyous cackles.

"He got you good, Auntie!" Georgie laughs, and Gwen nods in agreement, laughing herself.

Quickly changing gears, I laugh along with them. "Yep, he sure did." I shoot a quick glare over at Trevor—now a good ten feet away from me, smart man—who shrugs his shoulders with an innocent look on his face. Innocent, my ass.

The rest of the evening is much of the same. We splash around in the pool, the grown children—Alex and Joey—challenge the actual children to races and other water-based competitions. For the most part, I sit back with Evie and Ally and take it all in. The beauty of the surroundings...the happy sounds. I haven't seen Georgie and Gwen this animated in a long time, and I feel horribly guilty about that.

Alex cons Ally into a race; I'm told she was a big deal swimmer back in high school. Trevor is on the opposite side of the pool talking with the quiet one, Chase. Every so often when he looks my way and smiles, I melt a little more inside. I feel like a schoolgirl with a crush.

"I've never seen Trevor like this before," Evie says from her place beside me, startling me out of my ogling of Trevor.

"Never seen him like what?" I ask.

"So relaxed and content."

"He *is* on vacation," I offer.

"No, that's not it."

I know what she's getting at, but I'm not sure I want to hear her say it.

"He really likes you," she finally says.

"He hasn't even known me twenty-four hours," I argue, knowing full well I kind of like him, too, so that argument is moot.

"The heart wants what the heart wants."

"Heart?" I choke out in disbelief. No one said anything about hearts. Sure, mine might beat a little bit harder when I see him or think about him, but it's only been one day. Hearts don't get involved after one day.

Evie laughs. "That man has had goo-goo eyes for you all day long. And Trevor Monroe may be a big teddy bear, but he's got a tough exterior. You seem to have penetrated that. I bet if his heart isn't involved yet, it will be very soon."

"I sure hope not," I say honestly. "He'll be leaving after a while and I'll still be here."

"You know how Joey and I met?" I shake my head. "The band had a five day tour stop in Dallas, near where I'm from. When I met him, I knew there was something different about him. We spent those few days together, and we were both smitten." Her eyes are smiling as she watches Joey sitting on the side of the pool with Max, playing referee to Ally and Alex's races. "After five days, I knew. Less than five days, really. I couldn't let him go. I joined their tour; we got married a couple stops later in Vegas, and the rest is history. That was five years ago."

"That's a beautiful story, but I can't be that spontaneous," I say with a frown. "My business is here, and the twins. I couldn't just pick up and leave."

"I'm not saying you have to, hon." She pats my shoulder. "I'm just trying to tell you that anything is possible. Just keep an open mind. You never know what five days, or thirty, might bring," she winks.

Heartache, I think to myself. All it will bring is heartache if I'm not careful.

Chapter Eleven

Sara

The sun sets, and the kids are exhausted. Heck, I'm exhausted. It's been a long day, and usually by this hour, the three of us are settled down in our beds with our books. We've already said goodnight to everyone except Trevor, who is still here on the ground floor with us. Despite their obvious exhaustion, or, more than likely, because of it, Georgie and Gwen fight me every step of the way as I dry them off and get them dressed.

"But Auntie, they have a movie theater!" Gwen protests.

"We can watch a movie at home," I tell her calmly, knowing that when they're cranky like this, the slightest thing can set them off. I try to keep even tones and not over stimulate them.

"I don't want to watch a movie at home!" she cries.

Annnnd insert meltdown here.

I sigh and look at Georgie, daring him to make a similar spectacle. He frowns and looks down at the ground, but not before I see the tears well up in his eyes. They were having such a perfect day, and I hate that it has to end like this.

While I'm finishing up with Gwen, which has become quite the challenge due to the flailing limbs and endless tears, I see Trevor squat down to Georgie's level and speak to him in soft, quiet tones. The little boy looks up, smiles and nods through his tears at whatever Trevor is telling him. I don't know whether I want to hug the man for making him smile or curse at him for most likely making promises to a little boy that he can't keep.

Trevor looks over to me and smiles. I try to ignore what it does to my insides. I finish drying Gwen's hair and when I stand up, Trevor swoops in, picks Gwen up and tosses her over his shoulder—at which she giggles. Giggles! The little girl who was just crying like it was the end of the world is giggling.

And if that wasn't enough to shock me, Georgie plows into my legs and wraps his little arms around me. "I love you, Auntie. I had so much fun today."

I squat down to hug him. "I love you, too, bug." I stand up and take his hand. Trevor still has Gwen over his shoulder, but he stops to take the beach bag from me, and we all walk outside. I unlock the Jeep, and he sits Gwen in on one side, whispering something to her, while I open the opposite door for Georgie. We meet at the back of the Jeep once the kids are tucked inside.

"What did you say to them?" I ask, wincing at my harsh tone.

"Nothing bad, I promise."

"Look, you can't just make them promises you can't keep. They've been disappointed enough, and they'll be devastated—"

His lips suddenly press against mine, effectively shutting me up. His arms go around my shoulders and mine around his waist, holding each other close. The feel of his hard body against mine makes me moan. It would be way too easy to get carried away right now, but the twins are less than three feet away. Reluctantly, I pull away from him, disappointed I didn't quite get a taste of this gorgeous man.

He leans his forehead against mine and sighs. "I told them that maybe if they were good, you'd bring them back some day. That's all. I'm sorry if I was out of line. It just broke my heart to see them so sad. And I really, really want to see you again."

I squeeze my eyes shut tight, trying to block out the vulnerability I see in his eyes. Evie was right. He likes me. And if I'm being honest with myself, I really like him, too. He kisses the tip of my nose, causing me to melt a little more and then pulls away.

"I know this is unusual. I know we only met today and I'm only here for a month. I know all the reasons we shouldn't do this. But I feel like I have to do it anyway. Even if there's an expiration date. I don't want to leave here at the end of month and regret not taking you out."

I take a deep breath in, and exhale. "Okay," I say, looking into his eyes.

"Okay?" he asks cautiously.

"You can take me out."

He grins widely, lifts me up and spins me around. "Thank you," he whispers in my ear, his breath causing me to shiver. He puts me down and asks, "What are you doing for the Fourth?"

I shrug, thinking about the holiday tomorrow. "No plans. We close the shop for the day."

"So you have the day off?"

"From work, but I'll still have the twins. They don't have camp on the holiday."

"Spend the day with me," he says quickly.

"I'll have the kids."

"I don't care. I like the kids."

"You want to spend the day with two six year olds?" I raise my eyebrow. I don't even want to spend my day with two six year olds sometimes.

"I want to spend the day with you, and if y'all are a package deal, then yes, I want to spend my day with two six year olds."

And my heart is officially a pile of goo in my chest. I can't stop the grin from spreading across my face. "You've got a deal, Mr. Monroe."

"You don't know how happy that makes me, Miss Sands." Actually, I think I do know. Because I feel it, too.

We exchange cell phones and each plug our numbers in the other's, then part with a chaste peck on the lips and a promise that he'll call with plans in the morning. I don't want to leave his embrace, but the kids are in the car, and I can't exactly leave them in there and make out with him all night.

I drive away, grinning like a fool at the man waving at me in the rear view mirror. Trevor Monroe is like a dream. A responsible family man who loves kids and is kind, sweet, and gentle. Not to mention, he's sexy as hell. He's everything I've ever wanted in a guy. The complete package.

But he's leaving.

I'd be stupid to start something with him now, no matter how light we *try* to keep things because I already have the feels, and I know time will only intensify what I'm feeling after one day.

I'll just text him in the morning and tell him I can't make it, that something's come up. And that will be that. He'll forget about me after a few days. And I'll forget about him, too.

Who am I kidding?

I'll never be able to forget Trevor Monroe...

Chapter Twelve

Trevor

I wake in the morning completely exhausted after a night of restless sleep. Restless because I couldn't get a certain pair of ocean blue eyes out of my head. Ocean blue eyes and the most amazing kiss.

Sara.

Beautiful Sara with blue eyes, long, gorgeous brown hair, legs that go on for miles, and the softest, most kissable lips.

Sara.

Everything about her is amazing, and she fits in with my family so well. Her niece and nephew are adorable, but there's obviously something going on there...something she's not ready—or willing—to share. Last night she'd said that the twins have been "disappointed enough." I don't know exactly what she meant by that, but I'm not naïve, and I know enough about Chase and Joey's upbringings to connect the dots. The fact that she had them last night, and will have them again today, leads me to believe it's an issue with their parents. How parents can't take responsibility for their kids is beyond me, but I guess that's easy for me to say since I had the best parents a guy could ask for.

My breath catches and I feel a pain deep in my chest as I think about my parents. It's been years since they passed but sometimes...it feels like it was only yesterday. The bright, flashing lights...the sterile smell of the hospital...the worst news of my life.

As I rub my chest, trying to alleviate the pain, I feel a familiar burn behind my eyes and shut them tight.

I will it all away...the pain, the memories, and the tears.

I have to be strong for my brother and sister, and for Chase and Joey who loved our parents as if they were their own. I don't have time to get emotional.

I kick off the sheet and roll out of bed. I hear light chatter through the ceiling, so I know someone is awake. A glance at the alarm clock tells me it's almost 8:30. I haven't slept passed 7:00 in a long time; I guess I really had been restless last night.

I decide to take a shower before heading upstairs to join everyone. As I'm soaping myself up, my mind keeps shifting back to Sara. I can't wait to see her again today. I know we just met, but there is something about her. Something I just can't shake, and—if I'm being honest—I don't want to. I want to spend time with her and get to know her. In the back of my mind, a little voice of reason keeps telling me I'm foolish to consider getting involved—on any level—with a girl who lives over six hours away, but a louder voice is telling that one to mind its own business.

***

Fresh from the shower, I join the family upstairs. Everyone is up except for Alex. No surprise there, it would take an act of Congress to wake him up before noon—makes for some fun times on the road.

Ally is at the stove flipping pancakes and Chase is beside her working on the bacon. I'm surprised she let someone else in the kitchen, but it *is* Chase. The two of them are like glue.

"Good morning," Ally chirps from the stove. Chase turns and gives me a quick nod, focusing his attention back on the bacon.

"Morning," I say, taking a seat on one of the stools at the counter next to Max. His booster seat is tightly secured to one of the chair-back stools. "What's up, buddy?"

"I eatin' pacakes, Unca T," he says with a mouthful of pancakes and a face full of syrup.

"I see that, little man. Are they yummy?"

"Mmm hmm," he hums through another mouthful. "Auntie is da best cook!"

I nod in agreement. "That she is." Ally sets a plate filled with pancakes and bacon in front of me and ruffles Max's hair. "Thanks, kid." She smiles at me before skipping back over to the stove.

"When are you seeing Sara again?" Ally asks.

"I invited her and the kids to spend the day with us today," I tell them between bites. Max was right, these are yummy.

Ally and Chase both turn from the stove to look at me—Ally with a big grin and Chase with his eyebrows raised.

"What did she say?"

"Yes," I say, trying to hide my grin with another forkful of syrupy deliciousness.

Ally bounces on her feet and squeals while Chase gives her an odd look. Ally doesn't squeal.

I raise an eyebrow at Chase, and he shrugs. "You're guess is as good as mine, bro."

Ally rolls her eyes. "Can't a girl be excited her brother, the monk, is interested in someone?"

I nearly choke on my food. "I am not a monk."

"Might as well be," she mumbles, turning back to the stove.

I do not feel the need to discuss my sex life—or lack thereof—with my baby sister. I'm not a monk. I've gotten my share of action on the road, but I'm not even close to the man-whore my little brother is, or the choir boy that Chase is, or the monogamous family man Joey is. Speaking of...

"Where are Joey and Evie?"

Ally giggles. "In the shower."

I shouldn't have asked. "They better cool it or we're gonna need a second bus for our next tour to fit their brood."

Ally and Chase laugh, knowing it's true. I'm surprised Max has remained an only child this long. Sure, I poke fun, but I hope to have what they have some day—that undeniable attraction to another person where you can't be in the same vicinity of them and not touch them. But it's not just the physical stuff, it's the emotional stuff, too. Joey and Evie have it, and Chase and Ally do, too.

Suddenly Sara's face pops into my mind, and I have to shake my head to force it out. No need to go there. Whatever happens with Sara is only temporary—a summer fling.

The clock on the microwave reads 10:00, so I excuse myself to the balcony to call Sara.

Chapter Thirteen

Sara

My eyes burn a hole through my cell phone as I pace the living room. The small, offensive device sits on the coffee table, daring me to pick it up and use it.

I'm supposed to be texting Trevor to cancel our date today. Hold up. *Date?* I hardly think that's what he meant when he invited me and the kids to join him and his family. I am getting way ahead of myself. This is *exactly* why I have to cancel.

I pause at the table and look at the phone.

But I don't want to!

I'd really enjoyed spending time with Trevor and his family. They're all so friendly and so easy to get along with, very different from what I'd imagined rock stars to be like. The girls are great, too, and let's face it—it's not easy making new girlfriends. Ally and Evie immediately accepted me into their little circle, and I genuinely felt welcome.

I plop down onto the couch and exhale a deep breath.

He's only here for a month...less than that now. You can't get involved with a man who isn't going to be around next month; and you can't do that to the twins, either.

Reality can be a real bitch sometimes; slapping you in the face when it wants to make its point.

I lean forward to grab my cell off the table when it lights up, startling me.

It's him. Calling to make plans for today, as he'd promised.

Shit.

I swipe the screen to answer the call. "Hello?"

"Sara." His voice is deep and so, so sexy. How can I ever say "no" to him? How could anyone?

"Hi, Trevor." I lean back and tuck my legs beneath me.

"How are you?"

"I'm doing well."

"And the kids?"

I smile. He's so thoughtful. "The kids are great. They're upstairs in their rooms."

"Not getting into mischief, I hope."

"Now that you mention it, they have been pretty quiet." I stand up and quietly pad up the steps to peek in on them. Georgie is doing a puzzle, and Gwen is reading a picture book. They seriously are the best kids.

"Somehow I doubt those two get into much trouble," he laughs.

"You're right about that," I say, heading back downstairs. "That meltdown you saw last night is pretty much the extent of their bad behavior."

"Oh, well that's nothing compared to the trouble Alex and Ally caused when they were their age."

"Oh come on, now. You were what? Twelve?" I laugh, taking a seat on the couch again.

"Yep. And they totally cramped my style." He sounds so indignant, it makes me laugh. I can't imagine him having anything but love for his younger siblings. "I love your laugh," he says quietly, and I immediately stop laughing. "Sara?"

"I'm here."

"So," he says after a moment. "I was calling about today. I think we're just going to grill and hang out by the pool."

I pinch my eyes closed. This is it. This is the moment when I tell him I can't make it, and I close the book on Trevor Monroe.

So why can't I speak the words?

"Sara? You still with me?" Why does his voice have to be so sexy?

"Yes, I'm here. I'm sorry. I'm just a little distracted." That's not a lie.

"Everything okay?" he asks, sounding concerned.

"Yes, everything is fine." I immediately feel guilty for the lie. "No, that's not true."

"What's going on? Is it about today? You're not gonna cancel, are you?"

I sigh. "I'm just not sure how this is going to work, Trevor. I like you. I think you're a great guy. Your family is wonderful."

"But..."

"But, you're only here for 28 more days."

"But who's counting?" he says dryly.

"I just don't think anything good can come of this."

"How about a friendship? Fun? Adventure? Excitement?"

"That all sounds great, Trevor. But what happens to all that when the month is up? We spend a ton of time together over the next four weeks, and then you're gone, and there's a great big void in both of our lives where the other once was."

"We can keep in touch, Sara. I'm not going to Mars. We live in the same state. And who knows? After the month is up, hell, after the week is up, you may be so sick of me you never want to see or hear from me again."

Somehow I doubt that. I completely and totally doubt that.

"It's not just me, Trevor. What about the twins? We're a package deal, remember? They'll get attached to you and your family, and then you'll all be gone. How do I explain that to them? I can't expect them to have, or even understand, a long-distance relationship. They've had enough inconsistency in their lives."

"Sara, I think we're getting a little ahead of ourselves."

I scoff, of course he'd think that. Just because I'm trying to think before I act, I'm getting ahead of myself.

"Stop getting all huffy," he says.

"Excuse me?"

"You're doing that thing my sister does when her head is running on all cylinders. I bet you're even pacing."

I look around. I am pacing. I didn't even notice I'd gotten off the couch.

"Will you just hear me out?"

I sit down on the nearest armchair and rest my elbows on my knees. "Okay."

"I really like you. I know that sounds stupid since we only met yesterday, but I can't help it. I also know the situation isn't a normal one, with us living hours apart. I just feel like I need to know you as much as I can for as long as I can. I know that's selfish, so whatever limitations we need to put on this to make it easier, I'm willing to do it. I don't want to hurt the kids, so if that's really what you're afraid of, then I completely understand. I'll back off and leave you alone." He says that last part quietly, and it warms my heart that he seems to really care about the kids. More than Lucas ever did, and we'd been together for years.

It's not just the kids I'm worried about. Granted, they are a huge part of it. They need stability, and it would be irresponsible for me to bring people in and out of their lives. But another huge part of the problem is me. I know how I am. I go into things with my whole self, with my whole heart. After just one day I can't stop thinking about Trevor, what's it going to be like after a month?

"If we do this, we need to set some ground rules," I finally say.

"I'm listening." I hear the eagerness in his voice and smile. He's definitely all man, but not without a certain boyish charm.

"We're just friends. No dates. And I want to keep the twins' involvement to a minimum. They already love you guys, so that won't be an easy feat, but I don't want them heart-broken when you're gone." Or me, for that matter, but I can't exactly say that.

"I can agree to that," he says quickly, and I stifle a giggle.

"Okay."

"Okay?" he sounds surprised.

"Yes, okay." This time I do giggle. "So...what time should we come over?" I ask.

"Is now too soon?"

I full on laugh this time. "Yes, it's too soon." In more ways than one. "Give me a couple hours. I've got to get ready and get the twins ready."

"So I'll see you around noon?"

I look at the clock; it's 10:15. "Yeah, depending on traffic." Duck Road can get extremely congested at certain times a day—lunch hour is one of them—especially on a holiday. One of the fine benefits of living in a tourist destination.

"Take your time, seriously, and drive safely. I'll see you when you get here."

My heart warms even more with his words. Why can't this sweet, amazing guy live closer? Why does there have to be an expiration date, as he so aptly put?

"I'll see you soon."

"Be careful. Bye, Sara."

"Bye, Trevor." I tap the phone's screen to end the call and puff out a breath of air. "I guess I'm doing this," I say to no one.

Rising from my seat, I call up the stairs "Georgie! Gwen! Pack your stuff, we're going to Trevor's!" Their excited squeals validate both my own excitement and my concerns. I can only hope we all make it through in one piece.

Chapter Fourteen

Trevor

I feel like I'm experiencing déjà vu as I make my tenth trip to the front window. It's just after noon, and I'm like a kid waiting for Christmas morning. Ally is sitting on the couch with a magazine, looking up at me occasionally with a knowing look on her face.

Whatever.

I shoot her a glare as I walk past her to the back balcony. As soon as I step outside, I'm assaulted by the heat. It's much hotter on the coast than it is back at home. I'm on the upper deck, staring at the tree line for no more than two minutes when I hear a vehicle hit the gravel of the driveway. I nearly plow through the sliding glass door as I rush to the front of the house, ignoring Ally's giggles. I'll get her back some day.

When I look out the window and see Sara's Jeep parked next to the van, I can't control the smile that takes over my face. *She came.* I take off down the stairs and out the front door, then down the eight steps to the driveway.

I can't blame her for being reluctant. Our situation isn't perfect, and she has her niece and nephew to think about, but I can't help but feel a need to be close to her. I agreed to her terms—just friends and no dates—but I honestly hope that after a few days, she'll change her mind and want something more. Hell, I've spent one day with her, and I want more.

But, again, she has the kids to worry about, so I need to stop being so selfish and thinking only about myself. She hasn't flat out told me, but based on our conversation this morning, I'd bet money that she's the twins' guardian. When she trusts me enough, I'm sure she'll share that story. Either that or my big mouth sister and Evie will eventually pry it out of her.

I approach the Jeep just as she steps out and I just can't help it. I pull her into my arms and hug her.

"Hi," I whisper into her hair. She smells like coconut and vanilla. She smells good.

"Hi, friend," she says back. Her voice is slightly muffled by my shirt, but I can still hear the snark in her response. I quickly let her go and step back, waiting for her wrath...but she only smiles.

"Sorry," I tell her, smiling back. I don't mean it, though. Not even a little bit. I will steal as many hugs from her as she'll let me. Bottle those puppies up and save them for when we're apart.

A sudden knocking on the window breaks my gaze from Sara's ocean-colored eyes, and I look inside the Jeep's window to see Gwen grinning at me. I can't help but grin back. She's such a sweet kid; Georgie, too.

I pull the handle and open the door. "Hey guys! You ready to have an awesome day today?"

"I'm not a guy, silly. I'm a girl," Gwen corrects me, and I laugh.

"You're right! What was I thinking?"

"You probably weren't thinking. At least that's what Auntie Sara tells my mom when she comes to visit." My smile slips a little at Gwen's words.

"Alright, Gwennie. Out with you," Sara intervenes, grabbing Gwen's pink backpack off the floorboard. She doesn't make eye contact with me, just hustles the kids out of the car and then goes to the trunk to get another bag. "I didn't want to come empty handed again, so I stopped by the store and picked up an apple pie and some wine. Nothing says 'Happy Birthday, America' like apple pie, right?"

She's babbling and looking anywhere but at me. What Gwen revealed clearly embarrassed Sara, and I know now is not the time to ask questions. She'll talk about it when she's ready.

"Let me help you with that," I say, taking her beach bag and letting her keep the wine and the pie.

She smiles shyly. "Thank you."

I give her my best smile and gesture for her to walk ahead of me. Not only is it the gentlemanly thing to do, but it also gives me a nice view of her backside. Georgie and Gwen are already bouncing up and down at the front door, so I call out the four-digit code, and they argue over who gets to press the buttons.

"My bad," I say so only Sara can hear, as we both reach the top step.

"Kids!" Sara softly shouts—yes, she has apparently mastered the art of a soft shout. "Gwen, do the first two numbers. Georgie, do the second two."

I call out the numbers again, and the twins follow mine and Sara's instructions. Finally, the door is unlocked, and we make our way into the house.

"Why don't we unload everything downstairs, then we can head up and say hello to everyone?" I suggest.

Sara nods, and we herd the kids down the steps to the ground floor. The wine is white, so Sara places is in the fridge after setting the pie on the counter. I place her bag near the back door, and the twins follow suit with their own before taking off up the stairs at top speed.

"And I thought Max had energy," I laugh, staring behind them with awe.

"I promise I didn't give them Red Bull with their breakfast," Sara sighs.

"Just coffee?" She laughs, and I smile, happy to see the light back in her eyes.

"About what Gwen said," she starts.

I interrupt her with a finger to her lips. "You don't have to explain." She frowns. "This is only day two, Sara. You'll tell me about them when you're ready. When you feel comfortable and you trust me."

"I do trust you," she mumbles against my finger.

"That's really good to hear." I remove my finger from her mouth, itching to lean in and give her a quick kiss, but I know that a) I already pushed it with the hug in the driveway, and b) I won't want to just give her a quick kiss. So I take her hand and lead her to the stairs, this time walking up first so I'm not tempted to check out her *ass*ets.

Chapter Fifteen

Sara

The Fourth of July festivities at the JACT household carried on just as the previous night had. Lots of food, fun in the pool, great conversation, and three kids passed out before nightfall. Fireworks are prohibited in the Outer Banks, so they didn't miss anything, just a few amateur vacationers shooting off bottle rockets.

After loading the sleeping twins into my Jeep, Trevor and I exchanged a quick, platonic hug and a promise to get together again soon.

Soon ended up being three days later. Trevor had texted me an invite to hang out the next day, but work—and my need for distance if I'm being honest—caused me to politely decline his offer. After waiting all day Thursday, with bated breath, my heart leapt into my throat when my phone rang at 8:30 in the evening. It was him...inviting me to the beach. He said it would be just the two of us, that the others had plans to go mini golfing. I asked why he didn't want to go, and he told me that since he'd scored over one hundred the day before, he didn't feel the need to further embarrass himself. I laughed at that.

So here I am on a Friday morning, on my way to Trevor's house—Trevor's *vacation* house—yet again. Blowing off work, yet again. Not that Vic doesn't have it covered, because she definitely does. I don't mind playing driver today, either. Trevor and his family only have one vehicle here, and it's a mini-van, not at all made for beach driving. And honestly, even if he did have the appropriate vehicle, I'm not sure I'd let him drive. Driving on the beach takes an acquired level of skill I doubt the city boy has, not to mention all the rules and regulations that must be strictly followed.

I pull into the gravel drive, and there he is, sitting on the front steps in a pair of dark green board shorts and a white t-shirt pulled tight over his muscular chest and arms. His dark blond hair is messy and his denim-colored eyes are hidden behind gold-framed aviators. I can tell he's spent some time in the sun because he's considerably tanner than he was just a few days ago.

My eyes go back to his face, and he's smirking. My face heats up as I realize he's caught me ogling him. He slowly stands and makes his way to the Jeep. The hoard of butterflies in my stomach start a stampede. Just two days with this man and my body is reacting so powerfully to him. I have no idea what more time with him will bring. And today is one-on-one time.

I'm in so much trouble!

"Hey, gorgeous," he says after he opens the passenger door and hops in the seat. I'm glad he's turned away from me, throwing his bag onto the floor and adjusting his seatbelt because my face is definitely redder now.

"Hey. You ready for the beach?" *Jeez, I must sound like an idiot! Is he ready for the beach? Of course he's ready for the beach...*

"Hell yeah. I've only made it down one day. Kind of crazy to be staying in a beach house and not actually go to the beach."

"Well, there's lots of other stuff to do here, so it's easy to take it for granted." I back the Jeep out of the driveway and start us on our way.

"I bet you don't take it for granted."

"Hmm?" I briefly move my eyes from the road to his face. I shouldn't have...he's looking at me with such desire, it makes me gulp back a groan.

"I bet you don't take the beach for granted," he repeats.

"Definitely not. I love it. I've been a beach girl since I was a kid. I grew up here, so it's kind of hard not to fall in love with it. My parents had a home not too far from the beach, so my sister and I would go there almost every day."

"Where are your parents now?"

"They live in a retirement community near Rocky Mount." Talking about my parents is a pretty safe topic. I just hope he doesn't ask about my sister.

"That's pretty far."

"My mother's younger sister lives in the area and they wanted to be closer to her," I shrug my shoulders.

"Must be hard not having them close."

"Well, it's not easy. I'd rather them be close, but it is what it is. My parents are almost eighty, and the beach lifestyle isn't for them anymore. They had to go somewhere more practical for them."

"You ever thinking about moving closer to them?" he asks, and I get the sense he's not just talking about moving to Rocky Mount.

"The beach is my home. I could never leave here."

"Can't say that I blame you; it's beautiful here."

The mood in the car is pretty subdued after that, and maybe that's a good thing. There's no point in either one of us getting too involved—or excited—when things can't possibly progress beyond this month.

***

I park the Jeep on the beach along Ocean Highway, away from other beachgoers and traffic. We both hop out of the car and meet at the back to unload the blanket, towels, chairs, and umbrella.

"Man, I had you all wrong!" Trevor teases as he carries the chairs and umbrella to the soft sand in front of the Jeep.

"Oh, yeah? How's that?" I'm not sure where he's going with this, but I'll play along.

"You said you were a beach girl," he continues as he unfolds the chairs. "I figured that meant some raw sand and sun, but here you are with an umbrella and chairs."

"I brought them for you, city boy!" I tease back without skipping a beat. "Figured the sun and sand might be a little too much for you to handle."

"Oh, you did, did you?" he says back, stalking towards me with a glint of mischief in his eyes and a playful smirk on his face. I drop the blanket and towels I'm holding and back away from him, knowing whatever he's got up his sleeve isn't going to work out well for me.

"I was just trying to be helpful," I tell him.

"Uh huh," he pulls his shirt over his head and tosses it on one of the chairs while still approaching me.

Jeez, his body...

"Eyes up here."

My eyes slowly move up his body until they reach his smirking mouth and those deep blue eyes filled with want. Then I back right into the front of the Jeep. *That's gonna bruise.* I'd probably register the pain if I wasn't mesmerized by the needy look in his eyes.

"This is the part where I'm supposed to pick you up and throw you in the water," he calmly says, his face only inches from mine now. "But I won't."

He's so close I can almost taste the minty scent of his gum, and despite the heat—from both the temperature and the moment—my entire body is prickling with goosebumps.

"Why not?" I ask, breathless by his proximity.

He raises his right hand towards my shoulder and traces his index finger along the inside of the strap of my tank top.

"Because I'll get you all wet."

Too late.

His sudden grin makes me realize I said that last part out loud.

Crap.

Chapter Sixteen

Trevor

"Too late," she says, and then her eyes widen. Guess she didn't mean to let that one out of the bag, but she did, and I can't say I'm disappointed. My fingers are still toying with the strap of her tank top, and I want so badly to just rip it off, especially after feeling her shiver.

But I won't.

We agreed to be friends, and as much as I want it to be more than that, I have to respect her wishes. At least for now. I've got twenty-five more days to work on that.

I release her strap and reach up to tuck a stray hair behind her ear, taking pleasure in the sight of another shiver.

"Cold?" I tease.

"Uh-uh," she says.

Speechless. I like it.

I give her another grin and tip my chin towards the back of the Jeep. "Need me to get anything else out of the back?"

I can see the fogginess leave her eyes as she seems to return to her senses. "All that's left is the cooler, and we can leave that there. I just brought some water and a few snacks for later."

"Sounds good." I say, and we turn to walk back towards the blanket. She still seems a bit shell-shocked, and I love that I have that effect on her. "Wanna go for a swim?"

"Eager much?" She laughs, and it sounds like bells.

"I've been dying to jump in since we got here the other day," I admit.

"I thought you said y'all went to the beach already." She pulls off her tank top and I'm momentarily stunned by the sight of her nearly naked body. Her trim waist is punctuated with a small belly ring and she's tanned to perfection. Her...assets...are just the right size, too. "Eyes up here," she says, laughing.

I meet her eyes and smile.

What were we talking about?

"Did you not swim when you went to the beach?"

Oh right. The beach.

"I wanted to. But Ally started freaking out the moment our feet hit the water."

She unbuttons her jean shorts and my eyes fall to her hands, following the movement. "Is she afraid of the water or something?" she asks as she pushes her shorts down. They fall down her long legs to her feet. "I thought she was a swimmer."

I mentally shake my head.

What did she just say?

The water...Right.

"No. Well, sort of. Ally *was* a swim champ back in high school. But that was always in a pool. I guess with the ocean, it's more of a fear of not knowing what's below the surface."

Sara nods. "That's understandable. A lot of people feel that way."

"But not you." I smile.

She smiles back. "No, not me. I'd probably live in the ocean if I could find a way to pull it off."

"Come on," I say, reaching my hand out for hers. I feel a zing when her hand connects with mine. "Let's go get wet."

She turns about eight shades of red before I tug her along, and we run, laughing, into the waves.

***

As Sara sets out the blanket, I grab a couple bottles of water and the three plastic food containers from the cooler in the back of the Jeep. When I make my way back to her, she's adjusting the umbrella so it's acting as a sort of barrier between us and the group of people who had pulled in beside us while we were in the water.

"Want me all to yourself, do you?" I wink as I set the food and drinks on the blanket.

"A little full of yourself, are you?"

I laugh. I love how she can give it as well as she can take it. She doesn't treat me like a celebrity. That doesn't happen very often. Don't get me wrong, the star treatment can be awesome, but sometimes it's nice to just be Trevor Monroe, the guy...not Trevor Monroe, the bassist for JACT.

"If you must know," she begins as she settles down beside me. "One of the guys in the group over there had a JACT shirt on. I thought it would be best if you were a little concealed."

I look over my shoulder, but I can't see through the umbrella. "Good call," I tell her, thankful that at least one of us is perceptive.

"Is it difficult?" I raise my eyebrow, not quite following. "Going out in public? Getting recognized?"

I shake my head. "It's not so bad. I love talking to fans. They're mostly good natured, telling us how much they love our music or how it's touched them. Occasionally there's someone who also experienced the loss of a loved one and feel they can relate to us on that level, whether our music is their type or not. It's definitely cool. And it's not like we're Metallica or Guns N' Roses; we're not so popular that people will recognize us out of context, you know?"

She nods as she sticks an apple slice in her mouth. What I wouldn't give to be that apple slice. She licks her lips, and I look back up to her eyes. She grins and I wink. This flirting thing is actually kind of fun.

"So you already know a ton about me...and what you don't you can find on Google. Tell me about you. Who is Sara Sands?"

She rolls her eyes and lays down, rolling onto her stomach. This puts her perfect little ass in my view, so I stifle a groan and mirror her pose in an attempt to behave myself.

"What do you want to know?" she asks after a minute, seeming tense.

"What do you want to tell me?" I grab an apple slice and pop the entire thing in my mouth. For a minute, I struggle to chew the huge piece with my mouth closed and she giggles. Tension broken.

"Well, my name is Sara Sands. My birthday is this month. I'm a Leo. I love the beach. I own my own business. I'm blessed to call the two most adorable kids in the world my niece and nephew. My sister and I were adopted as kids when I was three and she was nine. She's my biological sister. I have no idea what happened to our biological parents, and I've never asked. I know it had something to do with drugs. Timothy and Margaret Sands are my parents, as far as I'm concerned. Nora, my sister, and I were never really close growing up. I guess part of that is because of the age gap, and I think part of it is because she remembers what it was like with our biological parents and I don't."

As she's talking, she drawing tiny little hearts in the sand with her fingertip. She draws a bunch of them, then wipes her canvas clean and starts over again.

"Part of me feels bad that Nora and I aren't close. But another part reminds me that she's the big sister. She's supposed to be a role model of sorts, and she's anything but. I tried talking to her about it once several years ago. It was pretty much the only time I was ever curious about our biological parents. It had to have been when I was like twelve or something. Anyway, I asked Nora about them, and she freaked out. She started screaming and cussing and throwing things. Eventually she ran out of the house. I hadn't realized it at the time, but she was already using then."

Drugs.

It doesn't take a genius to assume that's probably the reason Sara has custody of the twins. I take in the solemn look on Sara's face as she absently draws the little hearts and wish I hadn't asked. I want to know everything about this girl, but I don't want her to be sad.

"I'm sorry," I tell her. She shrugs her shoulders in response and just like that my probing has ruined our fun day.

Chapter Seventeen

Sara

And just like that, the depressing tale of my childhood has ruined our fun day.

Why did I bring that stuff up? Why didn't I just keep it light?

Because it's Trevor, that's why. He makes me so damn nervous and comfortable at the same time...the word vomit just pours out!

"It is what it is," I finally say.

"Is that why the twins live with you?" he asks.

"Yep. Nora lost custody about four years ago. They would have gone into the system, but I couldn't let that happen." I go back to drawing my sand hearts.

Trevor exhales a breath. "Four years ago? Wow. You were...what? Twenty?"

I smirk and glance at him. "Trying to politely ask how old I am, Mr. Monroe?"

"I'd never!" he scoffs.

"I was twenty-one."

He lets out a low whistle. "That's a lot of responsibility for a twenty-one year old."

I nod. "It was. But I was pretty much taking care of them all the time at that point anyway. It started out as a weekend here and a weekend there. Then Nora would *forget* to pick them up and a week would go by."

"Did you report her?" he hesitantly asks.

"No. At the time, Nora actually had a job, and the kids were in daycare. My parents couldn't keep a couple toddlers, and I had just started Sand Tours, so I couldn't take them during the day. Anyway, the daycare had been documenting small incidents over the course of a couple months. It started out small with her picking up or dropping off late. Some days they'd be dirty or still in their pajamas. They documented that stuff, but gave her the benefit of the doubt as a poor, single mother with twin toddlers. Kids get dirty, right? But then they were getting sick and their nutrition became a concern. They eventually reported her to child services for neglect."

"That's terrible."

"Yeah. Fortunately they don't remember any of it. I just wish she would have told me she needed more help. I was spread pretty thin, but I would have done what I could. Helped out here and there with groceries or something. So, she lost custody and I petitioned for guardianship. I had my own home and my own business, so I was stable. Plus, I was family. It was a pretty easy process. It became permanent after she was arrested for drug charges."

"You're pretty amazing, you know that?" I look up at him. He looks like an angel with the sun directly behind his head, forming a sort of halo. He is looking at me with reverence, like I am some kind of deity. I'm not...I'm just a girl.

I brush off his compliment. "I did what anyone would have done."

He shook his head. "Not just anyone would do what you did."

"You did."

He raises his eyebrow at me. "When my parents died, my sister and brother were adults, not toddlers. Though Alex is questionable sometimes..."

I laugh. "You know what I mean. You're like the glue that holds the family together. I see the way they look to you for guidance. Even Chase and Joey."

"I managed the band before we made it big...that's all it is." He excuses away the praise, but I'd seen enough when I spent time with his family to know that he's the patriarch. Doesn't matter if there's only a few years between them all, they respect Trevor and look up to him.

"So what's up with the hearts?" he asks, successfully changing the subject.

I look down at the myriad of hearts I've absentmindedly drawn in the sand in front of me and shrug my shoulders. "It's just something I've always done."

He focuses on the sand in front of him and starts drawing his own hearts. His are chunkier than mine and a little lopsided, probably due to his larger hands and lack of practice. I spend the next half hour showing him the proper way to draw a sand heart, and by the time we leave the beach, he's got it almost perfected. Almost.

***

After dropping Trevor back off at home, I head to work. I've got an hour before I have to pick up the twins, and I want to make sure paychecks were distributed and the payroll taxes were paid.

"Hey, girl," Victoria calls out as I walk inside. "I didn't expect to see you today."

"Just popping in to check on some payroll stuff," I tell her as I walk around the counter and open the office door.

She nods. "Everyone came by to pick theirs up. Manuel thought there was an issue with his, but I cleared it up. He forgot about the payroll deduction for the uniform."

"Figures." All employees wear a light blue polo shirt with the Sand Tours logo on it. I pay for the first three shirts, since it's a requirement, but they have to pay for any replacements due to their own faults. Manuel loses shirts at least once a month, it's not surprising that he's lost track of his deductions.

I sit down at my desk and wake the computer from sleep mode. Out of my peripheral vision, I see Vic standing in the doorway.

"What's up?"

"Aren't you going to tell me about your date?" She grins at me, and I roll my eyes.

"It was not a date."

"Please. Call it what you want. How was it?" I smile as I tap the keys to enter my password in the accounting software. "Sara!" She throws her hands up in the air. "Tell me. Now."

I laugh. "It was nice. We had a good time."

"That's it?"

"That's it."

"Tell me more! Tell me more! Don't make me break into song, Sara. You know I will." Victoria was in the theater club in high school, so I have no doubt she'll get musical.

"There really isn't any more to it. We went to the beach. We swam for a bit. We ate and talked. Then I took him home."

Not home, the voice of reason currently residing in my head reminds me. I mentally roll my eyes at it.

"So no more kissing?"

Ugh. I *knew* I should have told her that.

"No. No more kissing. We agreed to be friends." I will not mention the hot moment when we'd first arrived at the beach, and he nearly had me pressed up against the Jeep.

Vic sighs. "Oh, Sara. You need to live a little, girl."

"Live a little? He's only here for a few more weeks. Forgive me if I don't want to get involved in something I'm not going to want to let go of," I bite out defensively.

"I'm sorry, Sar. It's just that I haven't seen you look so excited about a guy since you and Lucas first started dating. And that was a long time ago." The bell to the front door rings, and she smiles sadly before walking back to the counter.

I blow out a breath. She's right. I *haven't* been this excited about a guy since Lucas. But it doesn't make a difference. In twenty-five days, Trevor Monroe will be out of here. And I'd prefer if my heart were still intact when he leaves.

Chapter Eighteen

Trevor

"Did you have fun on your date?" Chase asks, raising his voice to be heard over the low hum of the ATV's engine. We're currently parked on the beach while the other people on the tour are walking around looking for shells. Alex and Joey are still on theirs, too, goofing off and laughing amongst themselves.

"It wasn't a date," I tell him, thinking back to the time I spent with Sara yesterday. I wish it had been a date.

"Right," he smirks. "And I didn't pine away over your sister for years."

I laugh, thankful he can joke about it now. Those years he and Ally were apart had been rough on him. I can't imagine what it was like for him when he was the only one in the world who knew they'd been in love. It seems so obvious now, the way they gravitate towards one another. They're both lucky to have each other.

"But seriously, it wasn't a date. She just wants to be friends. We had a good time, hung out and talked. There was a moment," I didn't dare elaborate further on our moment by the Jeep, "but it was nothing. Strictly platonic."

"Strictly friend-zoned."

"And with good reason. I'm going to leave at the end of the month and then where would we be? I can tell she's not the type of girl who can check her feelings at the door...and she makes me not want to be that guy, either. She deserves more than a vacation fling."

I look over at Chase and he's eying me, carefully assessing in that way he often does. "Sounds pretty special."

"She is."

"So why couldn't you do a long distance thing? You do live in the same state, it's not like it's cross country."

"She's not interested in long distance. Plus, she's got the twins to think about. She doesn't want to confuse or hurt them."

I watch the waves crashing along the shore and the ocean beyond them. It's immense, stretched as far left and right as my eyes can see. The sunlit water reminds me of Sara's eyes and I can't help but think back to our moment yesterday. I can tell she'd wanted me then, but I'm not an asshole, and I won't push her.

"You know," Chase says after a few minutes of silence. "It's not like you need to be in Charlotte all the time."

I turn my head to look at him. "What are you talking about?"

He takes a deep breath, and his shoulders rise and fall with the movement. "I'm just saying that maybe you two could work something out. Sara is pretty tied down to this place, but you're not really tied down to Charlotte."

"Of course I am. The studio is there, and so is my family. You're all there. How am I not tied to Charlotte?" Why is he even bringing this up?

"Trev, you spend maybe a week in the studio doing your thing. The rest of the time you're just hanging out, waiting for the rest of us to finish. You don't *have* to be there for that. And if you wanted to give this thing a go with Sara, I'm pretty sure I speak for the rest of the family when I say we'd stand behind you."

"Stand behind me for what?"

"If you wanted to spend some time out here figuring things out," he quietly answers.

"I'm not moving to the Outer Banks, Chase. Sara isn't interested in a relationship. It's a non-issue."

Chase sighs and shakes his head. "You're so stubborn."

Maybe I am. Or maybe he's just getting way ahead of himself. I just want to spend some time with the girl. I'm not talking about forever. The suggestion of a long distance relationship—talk of the future in general—when I barely know her, and we've only hung out three times seems a little extreme.

Yes, Sara is different. Yes, I'd like to get to know her better. But no, I'm not ready to talk about moving six hours away from home—the only home I've ever known—to do that.

Shit.

So why is what Chase said making me second guess everything?

***

Later that evening, I'm sitting on one of the stools at the kitchen counter, watching Ally prep the shrimp for dinner. She seems to be enjoying plucking off the heads, peeling, and deveining them. It's entertaining to see her so immersed in her work.

When she'd first come home after her coma, before her memory came back, Ally and I sort of bonded in the kitchen. She'd always liked to cook and bake before the accident, and I guess some part of her subconscious had remembered that because she gravitated towards the kitchen almost immediately. She had gone through our mom's recipes and planned dinners and desserts, then she and I would hit the grocery store together. I'd never admit it to her or Alex, but not being one of the twins had me feeling left out on occasion. So it was nice having something that was just me and her.

"Chase told me what he said to you on the beach today," Ally tells me as she pops off another head.

"You're enjoying that too much," I say, trying to change the subject.

"He's right, you know. We only want you to be happy, Trev. I'm not saying you have to make a decision now, but if at the end of the summer you want to see more of Sara, none of us would hold it against you."

I rise from my stool and stand with my elbows resting on the cold granite countertop. "I appreciate the sentiment, but Sara doesn't want a long distance relationship. Even if I took time away from home to be with her, I'd still have to report to the studio and there would still be tours and band business that takes me out of town. It's not going to happen." I say that last sentence with finality, hoping she gets the picture.

She doesn't.

"I see the way you two look at each other when the other isn't looking. You're both into each other more than you're letting on...more than you're letting yourselves believe, maybe. I'm just saying that if it comes to that, you should consider it. Don't pass up on a good thing because of us. We want you to be happy. You're happy when she's around."

"I'm happy other times, too," I bite out, instantly regretting my bitter tone. Ally's just trying to help. "Sorry, Al."

"Just think about it, okay?" She smiles at me as she dumps the discarded shrimp parts into the garbage disposal.

I nod, pacifying her for now. I know she won't let up; she can be like a dog with a bone. But I'm not about to tell her that I have no intention of relocating, even if it's just temporary, to the Outer Banks.

Sara isn't okay with a long distance relationship...and that's all you can have with a touring musician, even if he lives in the same house. Ally should know that better than anyone.

***

After dinner, we spend the evening poolside. As I watch Chase with Ally and Joey with Evie, I can't stop thinking, *I want that. That happiness. That fun. That...love.* The peace of mind of knowing you've got a special someone. I've had my share of *experiences* on the road, but those were all empty.

Forgettable. I'm twenty-seven years old...it's about time I find something unforgettable.

My mind's eye flashes to a set of ocean blue eyes framed by gorgeous black lashes. Nothing with Sara could ever be forgettable. I bet ten years from now I could paint a picture of her face, even if I never saw her again. A few weeks with her would be better than never having her at all. And, who knows, maybe at the end of those few weeks, she'll be up for something more. All I know is that I'll regret not fighting for something with her. There's something there. She can't deny that.

Now to convince her.

Chapter Nineteen

Sara

"Can you excuse me for just a moment?" I duck out of our weekly Monday morning staff meeting, gesturing for Victoria to proceed without me. When I'd seen the number of the incoming call on my cell phone, I had to answer it. It's been three days and I'm jonesin' for some more Trevor.

As soon as I'm out of range of the meeting, I swipe the screen and quietly say hello, hoping the call hadn't already hit voicemail.

"I missed you on Saturday," his smooth voice states, causing a series of tingles up my spine.

"Just on Saturday?" I flirt back as I walk into my office. I close the door behind me and lean back against it.

He chuckles. "I meant that I missed you when we came by for the ATV tour." I frown. Well, I sure misread that. "But, if I'm being honest...I think I started missing you a little bit right after you dropped me off on Friday."

My heart flutters and my knees feel a little weak, so I slide down the door until my bottom hits the floor. My eyes blink a few times.

Is this real? Is he *real?*

"Sara?"

"Yeah," I say, cursing my voice for sounding all breathy.

"I'm sorry. I probably shouldn't have said that."

I smile. "Maybe, maybe not. But I liked it."

"You did?" Now his voice sounds hopeful.

I nod, then feel foolish since he can't see me. "I did."

I can hear him let out a big breath. "What are we doing here, Sara?"

I scrunch my eyebrows. "What do you mean?"

"I like you," he tells me and my pulse quickens.

"I like you, too," I say, waiting for the "but."

"But," there it is, "I don't know what to do with that. I can't stop thinking about you."

I squeeze my eyes closed. *I can't stop thinking about you, either,* I want to say. But I can't. Can I?

"I know the likelihood of this becoming something...bigger...isn't very high," he continues. "But I feel like I'll regret it—that we'll regret it—if we don't try. I know you don't want to do long distance...and I get that. It doesn't help that a relationship with me will always have some element of distance because of the band touring. But...I don't know...I just feel like it'll suck if we don't at least try. I've got about three weeks left here. I want to spend them with you. I'm just not sure I can spend another minute with you without touching you, or holding you, or kissing you."

I hear my pulse in my head, beating a steady rhythm straight down to my core. How can anyone deny this man? When he says all that...he wants to touch me? Hold me? Kiss me? *Ugh.* I want him to do all those things. Now.

But I wasn't kidding when I'd told him I didn't want to do long distance. If we do this...it'll be for this month only, then we'll have a clean break. It's the *only* way.

"Three weeks," I finally say.

"What?" he asks, sounding alert.

"I'll do this...we'll do this...for three weeks."

"What happens after the three weeks?"

"Nothing. When the three weeks are up, we go our separate ways." I hear him sigh and wait for his decision. I already made my choice. I might regret it later, but I want to have him now, while I can. "What'll it be?"

"Where are you?" he asks, and I hear rustling in the background.

Why isn't he answering the damn question? "I'm at work. Why?"

"I'm on my way."

I sit up straight. "What?"

"I'm on my way," he repeats.

"I heard you. Why are you coming here?" I get up from my space on the floor and rush over to the small decorative mirror on the wall. *I look like shit!* I run my hands through my windblown hair in a poor attempt to brush it, but quickly give up and start hunting for a hair tie.

"You just gave me the green light, sweetheart, and I'm not missing a second. I hope you've got someplace private there at your shop because when I get there, I'm going to kiss you so fucking hard you forget your name."

I freeze in my search and will myself to keep breathing. *Whoa.*

"Sara?"

"Yeah." My voice is all breathy, yet again. I clear my throat and gather up some courage so that when I speak, my voice doesn't crack. "Come straight back to my office, I'll be waiting."

***

Thirty minutes after I hang up the phone, there's a soft knock on the office door. I smooth my hair one last time and tell my visitor to come in. I frown when I see it's Jeanette, one of the girls who works reservations.

"Sorry to bother you, Miss Sands. There's a man here who says he's got an appointment with you. There's nothing on the books so I asked him to wait."

I smile, he's really here! "It's okay, Jeanette. I am expecting someone." She smiles shyly and nods, disappearing back through the doorway without another word. The girl is as sweet as can be, but she sure is odd sometimes.

Not even thirty seconds later, Trevor appears in the doorway. He leans against the door frame with his arms crossed over his broad chest, that devilish smirk on his face.

"Miss Sands," he says.

"Mr. Monroe." I smirk back as I stand up, then walk around to the front of my desk. I lean my butt against it and cross my arms, mimicking his position. I raise my eyebrow in a silent challenge.

His eyes darken, and he steps into the office, quietly shutting the door behind him...and locking it. I gulp. He looks like a predator stalking his prey.

What have I gotten myself into?

He stops just inches in front of me and his hands come up to frame my face. "Are you ready for this?" he asks, and I know he doesn't just mean the kiss. He means *this*. Me and him. And am I ready? I don't know, but I sure as hell want to find out.

"Ye-"

Before I can even finish the word his lips are on mine and *ohmygod!* I didn't think it was possible to beat the kiss in his driveway the other day, but wow. This man can kiss. His tongue massages mine perfectly, eliciting a deep moan from me, which leads to a groan from him. Our bodies are pressed so closely together, my arms wrapped tightly around his neck. I can feel the effect this is having on him. And this is just a kiss!

He is *kissing me so fucking hard.*

Just like he promised.

He slowly moves his hands from my face, tracing down my sides until he reaches my waist. He pauses for a moment before moving them around to my ass and squeezing. This time *I'm* the one who groans. I feel his arousal against me as he pulls my hips against his, and I'm pleased I'm not the only one effected.

Then, never breaking contact with my mouth, he lifts me up, his hands still positioned on my cheeks, and settles me on the edge of my desk. My legs immediately wrap around his waist, pulling him closer, and the contact of his hard with my hot center has me reflexively grinding against him.

He groans again, then abruptly turns away, stepping a good three feet across the room. I whimper at his absence, and he looks at me over his shoulder. The need is so obvious on his face, why did he stop?

"Did I do something wrong?" I ask, feeling self-conscious.

"God, no," he says, shaking his head. He comes back to me, standing between my legs, and lightly trails his fingers down the side of my face. "You're amazing. Everything is perfect. I just don't want the first time we...you know...to be in your office, and if I didn't stop then, it would have been."

Chapter Twenty

Trevor

The blush on Sara's face is so damn adorable. The woman is hotter than hell, but a little suggestive talk turns her redder than a tomato. I give her what I hope is a reassuring smile, and lean in to kiss her nose. She closes her eyes and rests her head against my chest, her arms now wrapped around my waist. I put my arms around her and hold her close. How she can go from red hot to sugar sweet in a matter of seconds blows me away.

I kiss the top of her head. "When do you get out of here?"

I feel her take a deep breath. "The twins have to be picked up at four, I usually leave here around three to allow for traffic."

I nod, disappointed. That's still hours away. It's not even lunchtime yet. And she's going to have the kids, so any alone time to talk about what exactly it is we're starting is non-existent.

"But...I *am* the boss..." I perk up, pulling back to look down at her. She's looking up at me with a shy smile on her face. "What good is being the boss if I can't blow off work every once in a while?"

I smile back, loving her way of thinking. "You'd be a pretty terrible boss if you didn't let your employees do their job occasionally."

"I agree." This time she instigates the kiss, stretching up just enough to wrap her arms around my neck and pull my lips to hers. She tastes like heaven and smells like the beach. I could get used to this. To *her.*

"You wanna get out of here?" I ask as I pull away.

She kisses me again. This time it's a short kiss, but she catches my bottom lip between her teeth as she pulls away.

She's going to be the death of me!

"Let me just go tell Victoria I'm leaving."

I nod and step out of her way, taking her place leaning back on her desk. I watch her

- 148 -

sweet ass sway as she walks away from me, chuckling when she catches me.

"I can't help it," I tell her. She just shakes her head, mumbling something about men as she walks out the door.

I rub my hands over my face and smile, pleased with the turn of events. I had no idea what kind of reception I'd get when I called her this morning, but I knew I had to try. I had to put it out there and let her make the choice. It's so hard to be around her and not want her. Now I don't have to worry about that. Now I *can* want her.

She returns to the office a few minutes later. "Where do you want to go?"

With her? "Anywhere."

She smiles. "I know just the place."

***

After a short drive, we pull into a gravel driveway. Sara drove since Chase dropped me off earlier. The house before us is an elevated two-story home with gray shingles and white shutters. It has a porch that appears to wrap around the entire house, and the open space below the house is surrounded by white lattice and appears to camouflage storage space and stilts.

"You live here?" I ask, impressed by the place. Sara smiles and nods. I knew her business was successful, but for her to live in a place like this...wow. I let out a low whistle. "It's real nice."

"Thanks. I've lived here for about five years now."

We get out of the car, and I follow Sara up the front steps. When we reach the top, I can see over the grassy hill that runs along the back of her house, and I see that she lives right on the beach. The grassy hill is actually a small sand dune separating her property from the beach.

"This is amazing," I say, distracted now by the ocean view. I walk along the porch to get a better view.

"It's beautiful, isn't it?" Sara says, startling me. I didn't realize she'd followed me.

"Yeah. I can totally understand why you'd never want to leave."

She smiles. "Go ahead around back. I'm just gonna grab a few things from the house and we'll walk down."

I'm not gonna lie. I'm a tad disappointed we're not going inside to finish what we'd started at her office. However, if I want this relationship to last more than ten minutes, I know we need to take it slow. I don't want to freak her out, she's already skittish enough about us.

I follow the porch around to the back of the house, occasionally stepping around a toy or a shoe the twins must have left out. The backyard is essentially an extension of the beach—more sand. The small dune directly behind the house steeps downward in the middle, making it easier to get from the yard to the beach, I suppose.

The glass French doors behind me open and Sara comes out, carrying a beach bag over her shoulder.

"I didn't bring a suit," I tell her.

"Afraid of swimming in your skivvies, Mr. Monroe?" she teases with a raised eyebrow.

I laugh as I shake my head, knowing she's joking.

"It's just a blanket and some snacks," she says, patting the side of the bag.

I take the bag from her and put it over my shoulder, then gesture for her to lead the way.

"Don't think I don't know what you're up to, Monroe," she says with a warning tone once we've descended the stairs and start climbing the small hill.

"Whatever do you mean?" I ask, staring at her ass.

"My point exactly," she says. I look up to see her looking at me over her shoulder. Caught. Again. Oops.

I grin at her and wink. "What can I say? It's a nice ass."

"You're so bad. I never would have taken you for a little horny perve."

I bark out a laugh. "Nothing little about me." She looks over her shoulder again, just long enough for me to see her roll her eyes. "Sure, we're all generally well-behaved, but we *are* still rock stars."

She laughs in response, and we amble on over the hill and onto the beach. I look left and right, taking in the vastness of the sea and the beautiful girl beside me.

The more time I spend with her on the beach, the more I find myself thinking...I could get used to all this.

Chapter Twenty-One

Sara

I hope I didn't give Trevor the wrong idea by taking him to my house. I've been with a few guys since Lucas, and I enjoy sex, but I'm not about to jump into bed with him the day we decide to give this thing a go.

He'd been mesmerized by the ocean view when we arrived, so I guess it's a good thing the beach had been my plan when I'd decided to take him here. I took him to the public beach the last time, and while this beach is still technically public, it's more of a local spot than a vacationer spot.

It's *my* beach...and I'm excited to share this little piece of me with him.

The only other bodies on the beach are about four hundred yards down, and it appears to be my neighbors and their kids. I see one of the adults wave and that confirms it for me. I wave back.

"Friends of yours?" Trevor asks once we stop about midway between the dune and the shore.

"Neighbors." I pull the beach blanket out of the bag he dropped on the sand and he helps me lay it out.

"It's much quieter out here," he observes as he sits on the spread blanket. "Aside from the waves crashing. Lots of seagulls."

"Sandpipers," I tell him as I take a seat beside him.

"Huh?"

"The birds. They're not gulls, they're sandpipers."

He nods, taking in the scenery. "You must know a ton running your tours."

"I do. I learned everything I could about the beach when I was growing up. I was fascinated by the sand and the water. The day I saw my first wild horse, it spawned a whole new fascination with the area wildlife. The history and lore of the area kind of went along with that. The tourism industry seemed like the best option for me. I didn't want to be stuck inside at a museum or stuffy place like that. I wanted to be outside in it all."

"It's amazing what you've built, pretty much all by yourself," he tells me with a proud look on his face.

"Well, my former partner sure helped. And Vic and the rest of the crew, too." I look away from his searching face, hoping he doesn't ask about my former partner. I don't want to talk about Lucas. And I really don't want to talk to Trevor about Lucas.

"So..." And here it comes. "Your former partner...when we went on the tour you said it was a 'he.' Ex-boyfriend?"

Damn observant Trevor. "Lucas," I finally answer. "The ex-boyfriend, ex-business partner."

"Must have been tough when you split up...having the business and all."

I let out a sigh. "It was very difficult." *In so many more ways than one.*

"I'm sorry; you don't have to talk about it." He puts his hand on my leg and squeezes in a gesture that's meant to be reassuring and to put an end to the conversation, but instead it makes my walls crumble a little bit more. Suddenly, I want to unload and tell him about Lucas. I want to tell this man everything.

"We were high school sweethearts," I start. "We started dating when we were fourteen and I thought we'd be together forever. Senior year of high school we started making plans for the company, even chose the name...*Sand Tours*. We took some business classes in college, just enough to learn what we needed to create a good business plan and get financial backing. Things were solid, stable...we were well on our way to making all our dreams come true. We opened the business when we were nineteen years old, just doing horse tours. We were surprised at how well we did, and we were eventually able to add more components."

I pause for a moment, because this is the hard part of the story. This is the part where love wasn't enough. Where *I* wasn't enough. Lucas had been *it* for me, but I wasn't *it* for him. I start drawing hearts in the sand—my therapeutic little outlet—before I continue.

"We had a great run for two years. I bought this house; he moved in with me. I thought we'd be married with kids by now." I shake my head at my foolishness. "Anyway, when all the stuff went down with Nora, and I ended up with the kids, he bailed. Said he wasn't ready for all that. I guess I can't really blame him. We were barely adults, enjoying our newfound freedom, and suddenly we had a couple two-year-olds living with us. He said he wasn't ready for kids and that I was only thinking about myself. That taking them in would ruin our future."

"He's an idiot," Trevor says, interrupting me.

I look up from my sand art and meet his intense gaze. "Maybe."

"No. Not maybe. He's an idiot. He had you, and you're one of the most amazing women I've ever met in my life. He let you go. He's an idiot."

"He didn't sign up to be a dad, Trevor." I sigh, not knowing why I'm even defending Lucas. He certainly doesn't deserve it. I guess part of me is still so terribly hurt that he threw away seven years so easily. It's not even just the relationship aspect, he was my best friend, too. Not only did I lose my boyfriend, but I lost my best friend.

"You didn't sign up to be a mom, and you're doing a pretty damn awesome job at it. All by yourself." I shake my head, willing away the tears forming behind my eyes. He lifts his hand and turns my face toward his. "You *are* amazing, Sara. You're a good businesswoman; otherwise, you wouldn't still have a thriving business. And you're a great mom to those kids, even if you're technically just their aunt. If I had a girl like you, I'd never let her go."

His words make me want to throw my stupid one month rule out the window, but instead I close the distance between us and kiss him. His lips are so soft, a contrast to the rest of him that's so hard and strong. He tastes like mint and I want to gulp him down like a mojito. He pulls away, but not before giving me two more small kisses.

"Hey, don't be sad," he says, wiping my cheeks. I guess I hadn't done as good a job as

I'd thought at holding those tears back. "I can't be that bad of a kisser."

I giggle, appreciating his way of defusing the awkward moment. "They're happy tears," I tell him, and I realize I'm not lying. They *are* happy tears.

"Hmm, then I guess we'll have to make some more of those," he says and he leans back in to kiss me some more.

We lay on that blanket, making out like teenagers, until Trevor's stomach growls, reminding us we skipped lunch. I drive us to a small café just outside of town, and we eat sandwiches and laugh about everything and nothing. When we're finished with lunch, I drop him off at his house so I can pick up the kids from day camp.

I had such an unexpected, fantastic day with him. I can't help but wish for many, many more days like that, but I'm instantly reminded that it's not possible. Then I push that thought out of my head and decide to do something different...something I don't usually allow myself to do.

I decide to live in the moment.

At least for the next twenty-two days.

Chapter Twenty-Two

Sara

"So how's it going with the hottie?" Victoria asks in between bites of her turkey wrap.

"I'm not sure what you mean," I say lamely. I know exactly what she means and she knows it.

"Oh, come on, Sara. I'm not an idiot. I wasn't born yesterday. You two have been spending some time together. You even blew off work the other day. That's not like you."

"I'm sorry about that," I say, poking at my salad.

She dismisses me by waving her hand, wrap and all. "I'm not complaining. You deserve to have some fun. You've been practically living like a nun since the twins came to live with you." I roll my eyes and she continues. "You seem happier lately. That's not a bad thing. I just want to see where your head is at."

"What do you mean?" I question, tilting my head to the side.

She lets out a long sigh. "You said he's only here for the summer?"

"For July," I tell her, and her eyes widen in shock, but she quickly curbs it.

"I just don't want you getting hurt, Sara. I want you to have fun and be happy, and if this hottie—"

"Trevor," I say quietly, looking around the small café to make sure no one is listening. Not that they'd recognize him by first name only but still. I know how he feels about his anonymity, and I would hate to be the one to let the cat out of the bag.

"If Trevor gives you all that, then great. But what's going to happen when he's gone in a few weeks?"

Nineteen days, I think to myself. He'll be gone in nineteen days.

"We've already talked about it." I tell her. "We're gonna hang out and...have fun...for the rest of the month. In fact, we're seeing each other tonight."

"And what happens when he leaves?" she asks again.

I shrug my shoulders. "Everything goes back to normal."

"And what if you're emotionally involved by then? What then?"

I set down my fork, appetite gone. "I don't know, Vic. I'm trying to leave my emotions out of it."

She shakes her head. "Sara...I know you. You *can't* leave your emotions out of anything. I'd be surprised if you weren't already emotionally invested. I know I encouraged this little fling, but I'm worried about you." I visibly deflate, and she sighs again, then changes tactics from preventative to aftercare. "Are you gonna be okay when he leaves?"

I shrug my shoulders again. "I'm probably gonna need a girls' night with lots of ice cream and wine."

"Oh!" she shrieks, drawing the attention of nearby diners. "They make wine ice cream! I saw it at the grocery store the other day."

I grimace. "That's disgusting." I like wine as much as the next person, but something about wine mixed with dairy doesn't sound appealing at all.

"I thought I knew you," she says, shaking her head with mock disgust.

"You love me," I tell her.

"I do," she smiles, then sobers up and reaches across the table to take my hand. "Whatever happens...you'll get through it."

I give her a small smile. "I always do."

"In the meantime, it'll be good for you to do the horizontal mambo with Trevor."

"Victoria!" I stare at my friend with wide eyes, heat rushing to my cheeks.

"What? It's the truth. You need to get laid, Sara. I just wish you could accomplish that without getting your heart involved."

I turn my warm, pink face down towards the table and start drawing hearts on the shiny surface with my finger tip. I can feel the eyes of other diners on us. Victoria seems to forget to use her inside voice quite often and there's a good chance the entire café just heard her talking about my need to get laid.

"I like him, Vic. But I'm not going to let my heart get involved." She sighs as I continue drawing hearts.

That's the first time I ever lied to my friend.

***

Vic and I drove to the café separately since I had to make a deposit at the bank and make a payment on my business loan. After I run my errands, I pull into the Sand Tours parking lot just in time for the delivery of some new kayaks. Kayaking is one of our newest ventures, and it's already getting a lot of attention. The twenty we had for rentals isn't cutting it anymore. This delivery will add another ten to our stock.

"Hey, Jim," I call out to the driver. He jumps from the cab of the truck, and I smile at the sight of him. Jim Porter is short, bald, and a little round in the middle. He used to be a lot more fit—he did decathlons and I think even competed in an ironman challenge once—but a nasty double knee injury he suffered in a fall during a bike race put a stop to all that.

"Sara," he smiles as I approach. "How's it going?"

"Great," I smile back, putting out my hand for a shake, but, as usual, he pulls me into a hug and I laugh. Jim and I go way back. He's been my supplier for our watersports equipment since Sand Tours began offering them. He's an expert and always willing to answer questions and give advice. He's been a blessing to me, especially since watersports had always been Lucas's thing.

"I can see that," he gestures to the busy parking lot. "Business must be booming if you're ordering ten more boats after I just delivered your first twenty in the spring."

I nod. "I'm surprised at the demand. We've had to turn people away, and you know how I feel about that."

He laughs. "I sure do. I'll get you unloaded and bring the invoice inside in a few."

"Sounds good. I'll send John out to give you a hand." John is one of our extra hands, here for the summer while he's on vacation from college.

"That'd be great." Jim heads back to his truck and I head for the employee entrance of the building.

"Sara Sands?" a voice asks. Startled, I spin around with my hand on my chest, trying to calm my thumping heart. Not sure why I'm so edgy, but this guy seems to have come from out of nowhere.

"Who are you?" I ask the man. He's tall and slim, wearing a suit in eighty-five degree weather. He looks a lot like Agent K from *Men in Black*, only more uptight, if that's possible. All I know is that if he pulls out one of those memory sticks, I'm booking it.

"Are you Sara Sands?" he asks again.

I roll my eyes. I don't have time for this. "Yes."

He reaches into his suit jacket and I take a step back. Maybe my initial instincts had been right. Maybe I'd been on edge for a reason. When he removes his hand he's holding an envelope, which he hands to me.

"You've been served."

My jaw drops and I stare at the offending envelope in my hand. It looks innocuous enough, but its contents...it's a thick envelope.

"What is this about?" I ask Agent K's retreating back. "Real nice. Just shit on someone's entire day and don't even stick around for the encore." I mumble to myself.

I tear into the envelope and pull out the contents. Several sheets of paper are clipped together. They're legal documents—obviously, since I was served and all. I skim the legalese, occasionally recognizing a word...*Currituck County...Nora Elizabeth Sands...petition for custody of Gwendolyn Marie Sands and George Edward Sands...*

Wait. *What?*

Chapter Twenty-Three

Trevor

It's 6:30, and Sara's late. I try not to let my nerves show, but my pacing is making it kind of hard to hide. We had a great day on Monday. We made progress. Surely we're not—she's not—taking a step back here. I haven't seen her since then, but we've spoken on the phone and texted. Everything seemed to be okay. She was just busy with work, and I was busy doing vacation stuff with my family.

I look at the clock. 6:31.

"Why don't you just call her?" Chase says from the couch where he's reading a book—a musician's biography, no doubt. It's how he'd kept his mind busy when he was apart from Ally, and over time the hobby stuck. He's got quite the library at home and brought a bag of them with him on this trip. I know because it was one of the bags I grabbed when we were unpacking the van.

"I don't want to seem over-eager," I tell him, looking at the clock again. Damn thing still says 6:31.

"Aren't you, though?"

I glare at him before stomping down the steps—all adult-like—and going in my bedroom to look for my cell phone. I locate it on the nightstand and pick it up. Tapping the screen, I notice there are no missed calls. No texts. Surely if she was going to stand me up, she'd text. She's the one who wanted to give it a go. She's the one who came up with the one month term. We just texted this morning about tonight.

Just call her, I hear Chase's voice say in my head.

I scroll to her number and dial.

She picks up after the third ring and sounds distraught. "Dammit. I'm so sorry, Trevor."

"Is everything okay?" God, she could have been in an accident or something! I didn't even think of that. What an asshole. "Are you okay? The kids?"

"No, we're okay. *Physically,* we're all fine." She sighs, and I can feel her tension through the phone.

"Then what's going on? Can I help?"

"No. Maybe. I don't know." She lets out another sigh, and I hear the ruffling of papers in the background. "I got served today."

Served? "Like legally served?"

"Yes."

"For what? Did something happen at work?" She has people sign those waivers, but I bet that doesn't stop them from trying to pull a lawsuit if they get injured.

"No. It's Nora."

"Your sister?"

"The one and only."

"What the hell is she suing you for?" No sooner than the words are out of my mouth does the lightbulb go off. The twins. Custody. "No. The kids? She can't...can she?"

"Apparently, she can. I just don't get it. Why does she even want them? She didn't take care of them when she had them. She doesn't know who their dad is, so it's not like she can get child support. I swear, I have no idea what goes through her damn mind. She's something else. If she had her crap together, I'd have no issues at all with her seeing the kids. None. They're her kids. I want nothing more than for her to be the mom she was supposed to be."

I take a seat in the armchair in my bedroom and let her vent. She obviously needs to get this out and if all I can be to her tonight is a sounding board, then sounding board I am.

"But she hasn't changed a damn bit. She had to have started these proceedings weeks ago for me to be served today and just ten days ago she was at my house stirring up shit. Real freaking mature. Real mom material, doing donuts in the damn driveway and scaring the shit out of her kids. The court must be insane to even consider honoring this request. How can she even afford to hire an attorney? I just don't get it."

"How can I help?" I ask her after a long silence.

"There's nothing we can do right now. I've already spoken to my lawyer. I gave him the papers. Everything is legit, and we just need to wait it out. I don't know how she can even petition a permanent placement. I have to appear the Monday after next. My lawyer is pretty confident her history will make a good enough case against her without having to come up with more evidence. It's just frustrating as hell. Why would she do this? Why can't I just have a normal sister?"

"Sadly, we can't choose our siblings." I wish there was something I could do for her. I feel so helpless, and she *sounds* so helpless.

"Like you'd trade Alex and Ally," she scoffs.

I chuckle. "You're right. I wouldn't trade them for the world."

"Must be nice," she says wistfully.

"I definitely won the sibling lottery."

"You all did," she quietly agrees. "Tell me something good."

"Like what?"

"Something. Anything. Your favorite family memory."

I smile. There are so many great memories to choose from, but I know just what I want to share with her. "This is sort of a memory within a memory," I start.

"Tell me."

"I was four when the twins were born. I don't actually remember anything from back then, but our mom would tell us stories about when we were little. My favorite was when she'd tell me about the day the twins came home from the hospital. It was the first time I'd seen them because I had a cold and they wouldn't let me go to the hospital. By the time they came home, I was better." I smile at the memory of my mom telling me this story. God, I miss her.

"They had me sit on the couch, surrounded by pillows. I was so excited, I thought we were going to make a fort or something." Sara giggles, and the sound makes me smile. "Then they brought in the babies. They settled them down—Ally in pink and Alex in blue—on each side of me and positioned my arms around them. I wasn't really holding them, the pillows were, but it looked like I was. Made a great picture."

"I bet."

"It's on the wall of our house. I'll show you some time," I say without thinking. I won't show her. Sara will never visit my house in Charlotte. It's likely we'll never speak after this month.

"I'd like that," she says, stunning me.

I want to ask her to please, *please* elaborate on that statement...but I don't. I don't want to ruin whatever this is right now.

"So, they settle these babies beside me, and apparently I'm looking at them like they're aliens. I'd never been around babies before. My parents explained to me that they were my brother and sister...that I was the big brother, and I had to look out for them because that's what big brothers did." I pause for a moment, having forgotten that part of the story. Is that why I've always felt such obligation to Alex and Ally? Because of my mom telling me this story?

"Seems like you've done a fine job," Sara tells me; I can hear the smile in her voice.

"Yeah," I say, my voice cracking with emotion. I clear my throat and continue. "My parents told me about how Alex and Ally were in my mom's belly, and now that they'd been born, they were going to be around all the time. By then I was mesmerized by the babies. Alex had gripped my pinky in his tiny fist and Ally wouldn't take her eyes off of me. I was awestruck. My mom said I couldn't—wouldn't—take my eyes off of them. From that moment on, I went everywhere the twins went, and I cried when we were separated."

"That's adorable."

"It didn't last forever, obviously. There was a short time in my childhood when I thought it was uncool to hang out with my younger brother and sister, but it was short-lived. Alex and Ally were cool kids. I mean, of course they would be, they had the coolest older brother."

Sara gasps, then in a squeaky, girly voice asks, "Is that your inflated rock star ego? I've been waiting for it to make an appearance!"

"My ego isn't the only thing that's inflated."

She groans. "That was just bad."

I laugh, loving that she isn't affected by my celebrity status.

"I'm really sorry I didn't call," she says after we stop laughing.

"It's all good. You had a lot on your mind." Sure, I had been a little annoyed when she was late, thinking that she'd bailed, but when she told me what was going on, my irritation vanished.

"Yeah, but we only have like two and a half weeks left. I don't want to waste time."

And there it was. The ever present reminder of the temporary status of our relationship. The disappointment I feel makes my chest hurt.

Distance, Trevor, I told myself.

"We'll catch up this weekend," I tell her, attempting to put up a wall.

"Yeah, this weekend," she says, her voice tinted with a touch of sadness.

I run my free hand over my face and resist the urge to groan. I don't want her to be sad, even though she's the one who made the stupid rule.

"How about I call you tomorrow morning?" I cave.

"Really? You're not busy."

"Nah," I lie. To be perfectly honest, I have no idea what the plans are for tomorrow. All I know is that I want to see her.

"Okay. I'll talk to you tomorrow. I really am sorry about tonight."

"I know you are and don't be. I'll talk to you tomorrow."

"Bye, Trevor."

"Bye, pretty girl."

I set the phone down on the side table and lean back in the armchair, staring up at the ceiling.

What the hell am I doing?

Chapter Twenty-Four

Trevor

Well, so much for not having any plans today.

At breakfast, Alex reminds me that we were renting jet skis today and taking them out in the Currituck Sound. Usually the things rent by the hour, but due to my brother's disposable income—he's paying for this venture—we have them for the entire day.

I'm a little surprised Sara hadn't mentioned anything about the rentals when we spoke last night. Then again, she probably doesn't have a handle on the everyday reservations, and she had a lot on her mind yesterday.

I'm bummed I have to cancel on her, but I promised my family I'd do this with them today and it *is* our vacation after all. A time for us all to relax and enjoy downtime as a family.

I decide against calling Sara and plan to speak to her when we get to her place. I just hope she's there.

When we get there, we follow similar protocol as the last time—two at a time. Alex and I go in first and approach the counter. He asks to check in, and I ask for Sara.

"Let me check if she's in," the girl working the desk says, looking at me curiously. I think this is her friend, Victoria, but she's not wearing a nametag so I can't be sure. She disappears in the back for a minute before returning with a knowing grin. "She says you can go on back."

"I'll be out in a minute," I tell Alex, and he nods, still focusing on the rental paperwork.

I walk around the counter and down the short hallway to her office. The door is open, and I lean on the frame, just watching her for a moment. Her hair is in a messy bun on top of her head and she's got these black framed, librarian glasses on that make her look sexier, if that's even possible. She's pouring over paperwork, invoices by the looks of it.

I knock on the open door, and she jumps in her seat, grabbing her chest.

"You scared the hell outta me," she scolds.

I grin in response. "Sorry."

She narrows her eyes at me. "You don't sound very sorry. I thought you were gonna call. What are you doing here?"

She doesn't sound pissed that I'm here. I take that as a good sign and step inside her office, taking a seat in the guest chair. "I forgot today was Jet Ski day."

She raises a brow in question. "Jet Ski day?"

"Alex," I tell her, as if that explains everything. She nods in acceptance, so I guess it does. I like how she already understands my brother's quirks. "He rented some for the entire day. Family fun and all that. I completely forgot about it until he told me this morning."

She frowns and I feel bad for breaking our plans. Or rather for breaking our plans to make plans.

"Do you want to come with us?" I blurt.

She raises her eyebrows. "For family fun?" she asks.

I nod vigorously, already imagining her sitting behind me on the Jet Ski with her arms tightly wrapped around me...my body

- 177 -

between her legs... "Sure, why not? I mean, technically you own the Jet Skis, so you can always call it work. Supervision, quality control, or whatever." Great, now I'm babbling like a pubescent boy.

"Well, I'll have to check with Vic. I did leave early yesterday." She furrows her eyebrows and starts chewing her bottom lip. I can tell she's running through the to-do list in her head. If Vic is the girl working the counter, I can pretty much guarantee by the grin on her face earlier that she'd help carry Sara out the door if it came down to it.

"So check with her," I say. I feel pretty certain her friend will be on my side.

"Okay, and I'll have to change. Just...stay here."

She gets up from her desk and moves to walk by me on her way out of the small room. I grab her hand as she tries to pass and put my other hand on her hip, guiding her so she's standing in front of me, straddling my legs. I smile at the question in her eyes, raise my hands to her shoulders, and gently pull her down so we're face to face. Her breaths are coming in small pants now, and I can't wait another minute before tasting those lips. I take her face in my hands, softly running my thumbs over her cheeks.

Then I'm utterly lost in her ocean blue eyes. Frozen in this moment.

Sara saves me, closing the small gap between us and pressing her lips against mine. Damn. It's only been a few days, and I've missed this...I've missed her. She runs her tongue along the seam of my mouth, and I groan, opening to let her in. I love it when she takes charge, lapping at my mouth. She climbs onto my lap, pressing her soft, hot center against my hard one. She moans at the contact and instinctively grinds up against it.

Shit. Two seconds of friction and I'm about to blow like an amateur. In my defense...it *is* Sara. I pull away, and she whimpers at the loss of contact. Or maybe it was me whimpering. I'm not really sure at this point.

Her eyes are hooded as she looks down at me, still straddling my lap. Damn if I don't want to just throw her in the van and take her back to the house and have my way with her for the next two and a half weeks straight. Or at least lock the office door for a while. But no. My family is waiting and this is her place of business.

I give her a quick kiss, because I just can't help it, and pat her ass. "You'd better go talk to Vic."

Realization dawns and her eyes widen a little. "Right," she says as she stands up and straightens herself out. "I'll be back in a minute." I lean forward in the chair, resting my elbows on my knees and my head in my hands.

What the hell am I doing?

I repeat my new mantra.

This cannot end well. This will not end well. Why not just leave well enough alone? Enjoy the rest of your vacation with your family and then go home. Get back to work. A few more months and we're back on the road. You'll forget all about her.

Right, who am I kidding? I'll never forget Sara.

The sound of someone clearing their throat breaks me from the downward spiral my thoughts have taken. I look up and see front desk girl in the doorway.

"Trevor," she says, walking around the desk to take a seat in Sara's chair. "I'm Victoria."

I give her a cautious smile. This woman makes me nervous. I have a feeling I'm about to get "the talk."

"It's nice to meet you," I tell her.

She makes a derisive sound, folds her arms across her chest, and purses her lips. Yep. I'm getting "the talk." I don't know why. I'm not the one who put an expiration date on this thing before it started. Ally and Alex aren't sitting Sara down for "the talk." Or are they?

"Where's Sara?"

"She went to change."

"Change?"

"Into a bathing suit. She keeps extras in the staff locker room."

I relax back into my seat for a moment, grateful that at least Sara's not getting the third degree from my siblings. I stiffen again when I look up and see Victoria's eyes narrowed at me. Her gaze is so piercing, I swear she's seeing straight into my brain, digging around for my intentions. It's making me uncomfortable.

"Sara told me you've been working with her here for a while," I attempt some small talk. Or maybe it's a diversion. Regardless, it doesn't work.

"What are you doing with her?" Damn. Straight to the point.

I let out a sigh and wipe my sweaty palms on my shorts. I've faced off against scarier people. I can handle the best friend. I think...

"I like her."

"She's been through a lot and I don't want to see her get hurt. I think a fling with a summer guy would be good for her, but honestly, I don't think she has it in her to have a fling. Sara cares for people...a lot. I'm afraid she'll get her heart tied up in this and then you'll be gone."

"I don't know what you want me to say. We just met. We have a connection. I like her...there's something about her. I don't know what it is, but I want to find out. Yes, I'm leaving at the end of the month. But I would like to have the chance to explore what's between us. Sara is the one who put an end date on this, not me. Honestly...I'm hoping that we'll spend this time together and she won't want it to end and she'll change her mind. I'm not sure I want it to just be a fling."

Victoria raises one eyebrow and considers me. "Look...Sara doesn't really have anyone."

"She has me," I interrupt, and she glares at me. "Sorry."

"Sara doesn't really have anyone," she repeats. "She's got me and there are her parents and the twins, but that's it. That's her support system. Her parents are hundreds of miles away, and the twins are six. That leaves me to look out for her best interests. Her ex-boyfriend was a joke. Her sister is a joke. And I'm not quite sure what to make of you. It seems you care about her— or are starting to, but I still see Sara getting hurt somehow in all this."

"I'm not going to hurt her," I say with conviction, pissed off she'd even suggest it.

"Not intentionally, no. I don't think you would. But...you're a rock star, Trevor. Sara and the kids...they need stability. They need someone in their lives they can count on. I'm all for Sara having some fun with you and then moving on...but if her heart gets involved..."

I can't argue with her there. If we chose to see each other beyond July, it would still be sporadic with us being long distance and me going on tour. I suppose that wouldn't be good for the twins.

Or for Sara.

Or for me.

But damn. How selfish am I to want it anyway?

Chapter Twenty-Five

Sara

"I'm all set," I say as I step into the doorway of my office. Man, I can feel the tension in the room.

Trevor immediately rises from the seat I practically dry humped him on and smiles at me. My cheeks pink at the naughty thoughts running through my head, and Trevor's smile turns into a smirk, clearly figuring out what's on my mind. Meanwhile, Victoria is sitting at my desk looking like the cat that ate the canary.

What did she do?

"Vic?"

She rolls her eyes. "What?"

I look over to Trevor. He's still smirking at me, then he winks and my core pulses. Big sexy jerk. He knows exactly what he's doing to me. I narrow my eyes at him, and he laughs.

"Hey, she was just giving me the speech, you know?"

"Uh, no. I don't know."

"If I hurt you, she'll kill me. That speech." He shrugs his shoulders like it's no big deal. And I guess for guys, it's not a big deal, rather a rite of passage or something. I'm still not sure I believe that's all that was going on because the tension seems a little too thick for that kind of talk, but whatever. I'm not about to start an argument now and ruin our day.

I pointedly look at Victoria, who still looks incredibly guilty...and surprisingly smug. How she pulls that one off, I'll never know. Her confidence is something else. "We'll talk later." She shrugs her shoulders in response, and I shake my head.

Trevor takes my hand in his and the gesture warms me. "You got everything you need?" he asks.

"Yep," I say, patting the bag on my shoulder that holds a towel, sunscreen, and a change of clothes.

He takes the bag from me and says goodbye to Victoria, even adds that it was a pleasure to meet her. Somehow I doubt that. I *will* be asking Vic questions later. But for now, I'm going to have some fun.

***

His family is waiting for us at the end of the dock behind the shop. Leah, one of my watersports pros, is just finishing going over the guidelines with the group. She gives me a surprised look and a small wave as she guides everyone to the Jet Skis. I give Trevor a quick run-through of the safety rules and tell him what the different buoys mean as we're putting our safety vests on.

"I thought you'd ride with me," he says, almost making it sound like a question. He actually looks disappointed.

"How are we gonna race if we're on the same ski?" I wink, and he grins. Oh my word, I enjoy seeing his smile way more than his disappointed face.

We hop on a couple Jet Skis and start them up. I tell him the appropriate speed to take leaving the dock, and we slowly follow the rest of the group out. As soon as we pass the green flag buoy, I let it rip. Looking over my shoulder, I let out a big laugh at Trevor's stunned expression, way back by the green flag buoy, as he shakes the water splashed up from my wake off his face and out of his hair.

I let off the gas and spin my ski around so I'm floating facing his direction. He gets a determined look on his face, pulls back on the throttle, and races towards me. I shriek and pull my throttle, spinning back around and heading out into the open water. I'm mindful of the other skiers in our area—not all of the rentals out belong to Trevor's party—and make my way to one of the far corners. I slow down a little bit as I approach Pete—he's watersports staff who sits in a rowboat in the middle of our section to keep watch on the skiers and to keep track of the rental times—so he knows it's me and doesn't give me any crap when I don't exactly follow the rules. When he nods back, acknowledging he's seen me, I cut loose again. Just in time, too, since Trevor is right on my tail.

I make it to the red flag corner buoy just moments before Trevor and clap my hands in victory. "I beat you!"

"That was dirty! I wasn't ready."

I laugh. He's a sore loser, but a cute one. "Hey, I even slowed down in the middle and let you catch up."

"You're lighter than me," he says.

Well, he might have a point there, but I'm not about to give it to him. "Are you always so pitiful when you lose?" I tease as I take in the little pout he's got going on.

His eyes narrow. "You're gonna pay for that. Best out of three."

Ooh, he's got a competitive side, does he? "I have something better in mind," I tell him.

"Like what?" he asks, drawing in his eyebrows.

I wink at him and jump off my ski into the water near the buoy. Once submerged, I reach under the buoy for the rope we keep attached. I have to do it quickly because my life vest isn't going to allow me to stay under long. Once I have it in my hand, I kick up to the surface.

"What the hell were you doing?" Trevor shouts at me when I break the surface.

I spin around and look at him, wiping the water from my eyes with my free hand. I lift up my hand with the rope, as if that explains everything.

He narrows his eyes, seeming confused. "Rope?"

Understanding his confusion, I quickly swim/paddle over to my ski and tie the rope around the ring on the rear to show him I'm docking my ski. Then I swim over to him. Finally, getting the idea, he holds on to the handlebar with one hand and leans over, reaching the other one out to pull me up. I get settled behind him and wrap my arms around his body.

His hard, hot, wet, half-naked body.

I let out a sign of contentment as I press my cheek against his back, and my hands around his waist, wishing like hell we weren't wearing life vests so I could actually feel *him*. He places his hands over mine for a moment and squeezes gently. The steel armor I've been trying to build around myself in his presence softens a little bit more at the gesture.

He releases my hands and puts his hands back on the handlebar, then takes off. We catch up with the rest of the group and spend the next few hours fooling around, riding each other's wake, laughing, and having an overall good time. We take the occasional break to rest the machines, have a snack, and get out of the sun. But I spend the rest of my time on the water with Trevor, only returning to my own ski when the rental time runs out.

I can't remember the last time I felt so happy...so free...I wish it never had to end.

Chapter Twenty-Six

Trevor

I part ways with Sara at the shop. She has to pick up the kids from day camp this afternoon, and I told Chase I'd hit the Wright Brothers Memorial with him while the rest of the group goes mini golfing...again.

I don't want to leave her, but I know she needs some space, and she's got to take care of the kids. Despite the fact I want to spend as much time with her as possible—alone at that—the twins come first.

After dropping the rest of the crew off at a new mini golf place—new to them since they'd already been to five different courses—I unload on Chase, telling him all about the custody situation Sara is in. I tell him everything I know, from when Sara got custody of the kids to her being served yesterday. I feel only a little guilty for sharing Sara's personal details, but I know Chase won't betray my confidence. He's my best friend, and sometimes a guy just needs to talk to his best friend—especially when he's got himself in a situation way above his usual level of responsibility.

When I finish the story, Chase lets out a low whistle. "That's rough," he finally says.

I nod as I switch on the blinker and turn into the parking lot. I hand the attendant the cash for the entry fee into the park and then drive on to find a parking space. The place is mobbed, but I spot a small sedan backing out and pull up close to take that spot.

Once out of the van, we note that the Visitor Center is pretty crowded, so we decide to check out the field and monument first. As we walk the path, noting the markers that indicate the length of each of the brothers' first four flights, Chase finally speaks again.

"Courts tend to side with mothers, no matter how shitty they are," he says quietly.

I let out a sigh. Chase would know. He ended up in the care of Child Protective Services once or twice when we were kids. His mother was no prize, probably even had Nora beat since Chase was stuck with her until he was old enough and financially stable enough to leave. At least the twins have had a reprieve—a chance at a normal life with Sara. Now they may have that taken away from them. The thought leaves a sour feeling in my stomach.

"That's what I'm afraid of," I tell him honestly. "I just wish there was something I could do to help them. Sara says she has a pretty solid case for continued guardianship...the same case they'd presented when she got guardianship of the kids the first time. But who knows what her sister has up her sleeve. I don't even understand why she's interested in the kids."

"They're a paycheck, Trev. If she has the kids, she can get entitlement money from the government. From what you just told me, it doesn't sound like she has any other interest. Hell, maybe she knows who the father is and is looking to get child support. It sounds like her sister is completely off balance, so there's no telling what her motives are, but it's likely they're not good."

I clench my jaw at the thought of Nora wanting the twins for a paycheck. They're kids, for God's sake. They're human beings. How people can use other people as ploys in their little games makes me ill—especially a mother using her children. Georgie and Gwen are great kids, they don't deserve that. No kids do.

Chase and I silently make our way up the long path to the monument. We're both thinkers and tend to work through our issues inside our own heads rather than out loud.

As a result, a lot of the time we spend together is spent not speaking. A fact the rest of the family finds a little odd, but we're used to it. We speak when we want to, but we know when the other needs the silence. Right now, I need the silence.

We walk around the granite monument and take in the inscriptions and the busts of Orville and Wilbur Wright. We fly often for concerts, award shows, interviews, and other industry stuff... it's easy to forget how it all started. These men were the pioneers of flight. Their efforts so many years ago make our lives so much easier today. Chase is into that—the roots of all things. I think that's why he likes biographies so much. Maybe it's because his own personal roots were so unstable.

I finish my perusing before he does, so I take a seat on a nearby bench to wait. My mind is still racing with thoughts on how I can help Sara and the twins. The truth is, I feel completely helpless. Whenever my family and friends had a problem, I was able to help them solve it. I'm the big brother, a.k.a. the problem solver. To be presented with a problem and not be able to fix it...it gutted me. Made me feel incompetent. Worthless. Useless.

I stand when Chase approaches, and we head back down the path to the field.

"You feel like hitting the Visitor Center?" he asks me.

"Maybe just to grab a souvenir for Max," I answer. And for Georgie and Gwen, I think to myself, even though I'm not sure if that's appropriate. I know Sara wants to keep whatever is between us separate from the kids, but a small gift shouldn't hurt.

Chase nods. "Good idea." We walk in silence for a few more paces before he speaks again. "What about talking to Adelson?"

Steve Adelson was a partner at the law firm with my father. He'd handled their estate and will, and he even helped the band with our recording contract. We haven't had to lean on him too much over the years, but he was always there when we needed legal advice. I hadn't even thought to ask him. The firm did a little bit of everything, and while he focused more on corporate law, he had dabbled in family law when our parents passed away because he and my father had been close.

"That's a great idea. Maybe he can look at Sara's case and see if he has any new ideas. Thanks, man."

We go to the gift shop, and I buy a blue airplane kite for Max, a green one for Georgie, and a pink one for Gwen. I don't miss the odd look Chase gives me when I pick up the extra two kites, but I do ignore it. He grabs a post card and a magnet for Ally, something he always does on tour when they are separated.

Leaving the park, I feel good. I have a plan to try to help Sara. It may be a small plan, and it may not work, but at least I don't feel so useless. I feel like I'm doing something. Something to help Sara. A shock runs through me as I realize I'd do anything to help that girl.

Anything.

Chapter Twenty-Seven

Sara

There's something I want to talk to you about.

Not quite the most ominous phrase in the English language—that award goes to "we need to talk." But this is close. Damn close. So close it has my stomach doing summersaults.

The twins and I pile into the Jeep early Saturday morning to go spend the day with Trevor and company. Georgie and Gwen can't stop talking about everything they're going to do at the "big house." He invited us over to play in the pool, go to the beach, play board games, cook-out, and for him and me to talk.

I'd be lying if I said I'm not terrified. Nothing good ever really comes of "talks." I mean, we're not exactly an item, so I shouldn't even be making a big deal out of it. But what if he's going to press me for more? What if he's ready to take this non-relationship to the next level?

Am I ready for that?

I'd suggested I was ready for more earlier this week, when we were alone in my office. I was very bold that day. But now...now my confidence is slipping.

Ever since I had that talk with Vic and got served, nothing seems right. Everything seems off. Like my world has been tipped off its axis. I still enjoy spending time with Trevor and talking with him. Yesterday on the Jet Skis was so much fun. Being with Trevor is like an escape. But that's just it...he's an escape, and soon enough, he'll be gone and it'll be back to reality...all day, every day.

As much as I enjoy spending time with Trevor and want—no, need—to have a little fun, I'm not sure I can justify it anymore. Things are already different now than they were on Monday. Now I may have a custody battle on my hands. Can I really handle a summer fling on top of that?

To be honest, Victoria had been right when she said there was no way I wouldn't let my heart get involved—not that I'd ever tell her that; I'd never hear the end of it. That knowledge shook me to my core. Even more so when Trevor called me the night I was served, and the sound of his voice alone seemed to soothe me.

I want him, but I know I shouldn't. I'm in way over my head. I don't think I'm mature enough to deal with this. One crisis at a time.

But that's the thing. Trevor isn't a crisis. He's a balm for my soul. *The* balm for my soul.

Temporarily.

***

Just after lunch, while the twins are occupied in the pool with Ally, Evie, Chase, and Max, Trevor takes my hand and tugs me around to the side of the house.

"Where are we going?" I ask, looking over my shoulder to double-check that the twins are being watched.

As soon as we're out of eyesight, Trevor turns and presses me against the side of the house. He places his hands on my cheeks and leans his forehead against mine, exhaling his minty breath right onto my lips.

"I've been wanting to do this all day," he says right before he presses his lips against mine. My mouth opens on a sigh…kissing him feels so damn good. He takes advantage of the opening and slips his tongue between my lips. I touch his tongue with mine and get lost in the spark.

Where are my reservations about all this? They took one look at Trevor's hot, muscular form in board shorts and flew the coop, that's where they are. So much for self-preservation. I am lost to this man.

His entire body is pressed firmly against mine as his hands finally start moving down...down passed my shoulders, whispering lightly along my arms, leaving goosebumps in their wake before finally landing low on my hips. I can feel the effect this—*this kiss*—is having on him and I whimper as he grinds himself against me. He groans in response, and his hands squeeze me tight as he lifts me up. Instinctively, I wrap my legs around his waist and moan at the new contact, grinding once for good measure. Okay, twice. Still lip locked, he moves his right leg forward and his left hand stays firmly in place on my ass, keeping me balanced. He then moves his right hand up and over my thigh, towards my center. If he makes it there, he'll know just how much I want him.

I want him...so badly...and if it weren't for the sudden sound of children's laughter, I have no doubt I would have let him take me right there on the side of the house. Just twenty feet away from our families.

Ohmygod.

Panting, we break apart. We're no longer physically attached at the mouth, but we are lost in each other's eyes. In his, I see pure desire, and maybe a little bit of something else I'm not going to think about right now—or ever. I'm sure he sees the same in mine. Some things are hard to hide.

He lets me down without saying a word, and I awkwardly stand before him, wobbling a little. He reaches out a hand to steady me.

"Let's go to the beach. We can talk there," he says, breaking the silence.

"The twins—" I start, twisting my hands in front of me.

"Are fine. Ally and Evie won't let them out of their sight. Just for a few minutes, I promise. Then we'll come back and get the kids and fly those kites on the beach." It had been incredibly sweet of him to buy them gifts, even though I told him it was completely unnecessary. He ignored me, though.

He takes both of my small hands in his one large one and tugs me further down the side of the house until we reach a small alcove where a little golf cart is parked. "We'll be quick," he promises as he helps me into the passenger seat. After giving me a quick peck on the lips, he jogs around to the driver's seat.

I twist my hands together. *Great, we're going to have* the talk *now.*

"What's going on in there? What are you thinking about?" Trevor asks once he has steered us out into the street. The drive to the beach isn't long...really, we could have walked. But the cool, ocean breeze whipping through my hair does feel good.

"Nothing," I lie.

"Sara...we may not have known each other long, but you have some pretty easy tells."

"I do not."

"You're twisting your hands," he tells me.

I look down at my hands, wringing together in my lap. Well, shit. I immediately stop. "That's nothing," I laugh it off, but even my laughter sounds shrill and off.

"Sara," he reaches over and takes my hand, "everything is okay now, and everything is going to be okay."

"You have no right to make statements like that," I say coldly, snatching my hand away from him.

"Whoa," he says, parking the cart near the trail to the beach. "What just happened here?"

I let out a sigh. "I don't know. I'm sorry. I'm just on edge. Everything was so perfect and now it's not. I'm afraid I'm not good company."

"You're always good company. And you're allowed to have off days. Sadly, things can't be perfect all the time, but we can always find ways to make those unperfect days better."

"I'm not sure 'unperfect' is a word," I laugh, trying to lighten the dense mood I'd just created.

"I've written a song or two, so I think I know more about the English language than you do. And since I've written songs, it means I can create new words. It's a thing."

I giggle at the serious look on his face. "Uh huh."

"Come on," he says, smiling at me and tentatively reaching out his hand. I take it and let him pull me out his side of the golf cart.

We silently walk hand-in-hand down the short grassy trail to the beach. The moment my feet hit the warm sand, I feel like I'm home. I close my eyes and pause for a moment, causing Trevor to stumble a little since we're still attached at the hand. When I open my eyes again, he's looking at me with that look again...the desire and something else look. He gives me a small smile before turning his head and tugging me along.

The silence is killing me!

"Okay, Trevor." I stop walking and tug him to a stop just before we reach the shoreline. "You're seriously freaking me out. What do we need to talk about?"

He looks at me, seeming a little shocked by my outburst. He turns to face me, taking both my hands in his. "Don't freak out, pretty girl."

This is not helping. "What do you want to talk about?" I ask again.

"It's really not a big deal, I'm sorry if I freaked you out or got you thinking something was wrong. I just brought you down here because I didn't want to talk about it in front of the kids...I wasn't sure how much they knew."

"How much they know about what?" Why can't he just spit it out?

"About the custody stuff. About Nora..."

What? "I don't understand."

"I wanted to talk to you about that. I had an idea. Something that may help. I don't know. Seems kinda dumb now, but I'm a fixer, you know? When someone I care about has a problem, I try to help." He's babbling now, rubbing the back of his neck and staring off in the distance. He's nervous, and it's adorable. Seeing vulnerability in a confident rock star is pretty sexy.

And wait...let's back up a minute. Someone he cares about?

"I'm someone you care about?"

He looks back at me and nods. "Yeah. Of course. I care about you and the twins. Did you ever doubt that?"

I honestly haven't given it much thought. Caring equals feelings, and I'm trying to leave those at home. I simply shrug in response.

"So what's your idea?"

He sighs. "It's nothing big, but I thought maybe you could have my lawyer look at your case. I'm not suggesting your lawyer isn't any good, but maybe a second set of eyes will pick up on something new...or maybe he'll have a fresh idea."

"Couldn't hurt, I suppose. But I really can't afford a second lawyer."

Trevor shook his head. "He's a family friend. He practiced with my dad. He wouldn't charge us for a consult."

I don't miss the way Trevor says "us" as though we're a team. Like it's me and him versus the world. How awesome it would be to be part of an "us" again.

Chapter Twenty-Eight

Sara

When we return to the house, Trevor leads me to the backyard where everyone is still playing in the pool. *The kids are going to prune*, I think to myself, but they're having so much fun I decide not to say anything.

"We're going to go inside and make a phone call," Trevor announces and pulls me towards the house.

"Right now?" I ask, surprised. I knew he said we'd talk to his lawyer, but that's awfully fast. Not to mention it's Saturday.

"No time like the present," Trevor answers. "And the kids are occupied at the moment."

The girls giggle, and I know why. I know exactly what this looks like...Trevor practically dragging me into the house for a "phone call." Yeah, I wouldn't believe it either.

He guides me up the stairs to the middle floor and into one of the bedrooms. He takes a seat at the small table by the window and motions for me to sit across from him. Looking to my left, I see that the window overlooks the pool. I can see the twins splashing around with everyone. Alex and Joey have since joined them in the water.

"Mr. Adelson is a really nice guy. We'll just tell him what's going on and see what he suggests." Trevor taps around on his phone screen, then sets the phone on the table as it starts to ring through the speaker.

"Trevor, I thought you were on vacation," a warm voice answers.

"Hey, Mr. Adelson. I am on vacation."

"Then why are you calling up an old man on a Saturday? And I told you to call me Steve."

"Sorry, force of habit," Trevor laughs. I can tell he has a great rapport with this man...that they're close. "Look, I've got a friend who could use some advice."

"I figured it wasn't a social call," Mr. Adelson says.

"Sara is here with me now. We're on speaker. I'll let her explain her situation to you and maybe you can see if there's anything her lawyer didn't already think of."

"Alright. Hello, Sara."

"Hi, Mr. Adelson," I say shyly, a little nervous that I'm about to unload all my drama on a complete stranger.

"Tell me what's going on," he says in that same warm tone he'd greeted Trevor with.

Trevor reaches across the table and takes my hand, instantly making me feel better. He gives me a smile and a nod, silently letting me know it's okay for me to talk to this man.

I take a deep breath and tell Mr. Adelson everything. I start with Nora's behavior back before the twins were even born, and I end with the most recent events—donuts in my driveway—only a week or so ago. I tell him about being granted guardianship of the twins when Nora was deemed unfit, and again when she went to jail. I also include everything my lawyer used in both of the previous cases. By the time I'm finished half-an-hour later, I'm certain there isn't anything he doesn't know.

Mr. Adelson is quiet for a moment, but over the line I can hear what sounds like pen on paper. Finally, he sighs.

"Well, Sara. Seems like you've got yourself a good attorney there. I can't think of anything he hasn't already taken care of. Now I'm sure Trevor told you, family law is not my area of expertise, but it all seems pretty straightforward, and it sounds like you've got your bases covered. Unfortunately, in cases like this, courts believe in second chances...particularly when it comes to biological parents...but especially mothers."

I swear I can hear my heart break. Of course, this is what I'd expected to hear, but that tiny glimmer of hope is squashed.

"It'll also give her a chance to screw up."

My eyes widen as I glare at the phone. Did I hear him correctly? "Screw up?" Trevor and I both ask. I look up at him, and he squeezes the hand he's still holding.

"Look, with your sister's history, she's bound to screw up again. I'm all for second chances and believing in the inherent good in people and their ability to change. But Nora's last immature act was less than two weeks ago. I don't know your sister, Sara, but I don't think she's turned her act around in ten days. She's bound to screw up. It's not likely that the court will give her a third chance. Or a fourth, in her case."

"I just wish the twins wouldn't be stuck in the middle of it. When she screws up, because as you said, I'm certain she will, they'll be caught in the crossfire. I just wish there was a way to ensure their safety."

"From what you told me, it sounds like that's part of your lawyer's argument. It's extremely likely that if she's granted custody, she'll have visits from a social worker before she takes custody of the kids, and while she has them."

I appreciate the notion, but it still doesn't make me feel any better. In fact, I feel pretty queasy right about now. Everything is becoming more and more real. One week from Monday and things may be very different.

We say goodbye to Mr. Adelson—who still insists we call him Steve—and before we hang up, I agree to his suggestion of telling the kids about Nora so they aren't blindsided. I scold myself for not thinking of that sooner. Of course, I need to mentally prepare them for the worst. I want them to be as comfortable as possible if we have to transition.

Once the call is disconnected, my shoulders slump, and I completely deflate.

"I'm sorry, babe," Trevor says softly. "I hoped he would have better news."

I shook my head. "Not your fault. I appreciate his opinion, and he brought up some stuff I hadn't considered. I really need to tell the kids."

"Want help?"

I look into his navy colored eyes and see the compassion there. It makes me want to cry. It also makes me want to lean on someone other than myself. I can't do that, though. I can't count on someone who I know won't be around for the long haul. What's the point?

"Thanks, but I think it'll be better if it's just me and them. I don't want to confuse them any more than they'll already be."

He nods with a faraway look on his face, then looks at the time on his phone. "It's about time to fire up the grill, you ready to head down?"

"Yeah," I say, standing up. "Can I use your restroom? I'll meet you outside."

Trevor stands up and pulls me into his arms, giving me a gentle kiss on my forehead. He points to the bathroom door and steps out of the room. I watch him walk away, and only when I hear his footsteps on the stairs do I head for the bathroom.

After using the facilities, I splash some water on my face and look in the mirror. Sad, tired eyes look back at me.

What will I do if I lose them? I can't lose them. They're part of me now.

I shake my head, splashing more water on my face. I plaster on my happy face—one I've had to fake many times for the twins' benefit—and leave the bathroom. I coach myself with happy thoughts as I walk down the stairs and head towards the backyard.

I pause at the back door and watch Georgie and Gwen jump into the pool and swim to Ally and Chase. Max is in Joey's arms, yelling, "Again, again!"

As I step outside, Georgie and Gwen see me and together they yell. "Auntie, watch this!" Then they jump into the pool.

When they resurface, I clap and cheer...ooh and ahh...and do all the appropriate proud mommy things.

Only I'm not their mom.

And that small detail has never been made clearer to me as it has these past few days.

Chapter Twenty-Nine

Trevor

Yesterday was rough.

After the phone call with Adelson, I'd felt even more helpless than before. The information wasn't new. It was all stuff her attorney had already told her. But I could see she had hope. I could also see the moment that hope died out. It was as though the light went out of her eyes.

Before she left, I begged her to let me spend the day with her and the kids. I could tell she was reluctant...especially since the kids would see me two days in a row, and she said early on that she didn't want them to get too used to me being around. Can't say that didn't hurt, but it's what's best for the kids and Sara knows best. I won't argue that. After many minutes of my saddest, puppy dog eyes, she finally giggled and caved.

I'm bringing them lunch, and I'm actually nervous. Sara had planned to have "the talk" with the kids this morning. I have no idea what I'm about to walk into. Chase drops me off at her house—this one car thing is really starting to get old—and I cautiously make my way up the steps. I don't know why I'm so worried about it. Maybe it's because I can't bear the thought of seeing those kids upset...or broken. If I feel this way after only knowing them a few days, I can't imagine how Sara feels.

Being a grown up sucks sometimes.

I give myself a little pep talk, then knock on the door. After a minute, a somber Sara opens it. This is not good. "Hey, pretty girl," I say, leaning in to give her a kiss on the cheek.

"Hey," she says, giving me a small smile. Despite the obvious stress and worry on her face, she still looks beautiful. She's wearing a pale blue sundress with very thin straps. It doesn't appear she's wearing a bra, I note. *What else isn't she wearing under that thing?* This woman is going to be the death of me.

I lift up the basket Ally loaded up with treats. "I brought lunch."

"Come on in," she says monotonously, opening the door wider to let me in. "We'll take it to the kitchen."

"Where are the kids?" I ask, noticing their absence immediately.

She frowns. "In their rooms...reading."

"Didn't go so well, huh?" I ask, settling the basket on the kitchen island and putting my arms around her. She rests her head on my chest and lets out a deep breath.

"It went okay. They're just really confused. I think they think Nora is coming to live here. I think I screwed the whole thing up."

"Nah. I'm sure you didn't screw anything up. It's not an easy situation, and it's certainly not easy to explain it without scaring them."

"I guess," she says quietly. I hear her sniffle, and it breaks my heart. I don't want her to be sad. "What's that smell?" she asks, surprising me. I pull away and look at her face. She's not crying. She wasn't sniffling, I realize, she was smelling.

"Um, Ally made chicken salad sandwiches and a whole bunch of other cra-, uh, stuff."

She quirks an eyebrow at me. "Nice save."

I grin. Her sassiness seems to be coming back. That's a good sign. "Want me to get the kids?"

She chews her lower lip for a good thirty seconds before she answers me. "No, I'll go get them. Why don't you unload all these goodies? Ally is an amazing cook; I can't wait to see what all that crap is."

I laugh and shake my head as she winks and walks out of the kitchen. I'm happy to see she's a bit more chipper now than when I first got here. The more time I spend with Sara, the more I get the feeling she doesn't do much for herself. Her life seems to revolve around her business and the twins. She does a great job taking care of those things, but who takes care of her?

Sound familiar?

Isn't that what I do? Put everything and everyone ahead of myself?

Sara and I may have more in common than I'd originally thought.

***

We had a fun time with the kids. It started raining shortly after lunch, so we made a day out of board games and movies. The games and movies did a lot to brighten their spirits...kids can be so resilient. I just hope Georgie and Gwen's resiliency doesn't get tested in the coming months.

After the second movie, the kids go to bed, and Sara suggests we head down to the beach.

"What about the kids?"

"They know I come down to the beach a lot at night. If they wake up and I'm not there, they'll flip the patio light three times." She shrugs. "It's our code. But trust me, they're in their deepest sleep when they first go down. I won't hear from them for hours, if at all."

She grabs a blanket by the back door and I follow her outside and down the short trail to the sand. When we were out here the other day, I hadn't realized the beach is only about twenty paces from her back steps. She truly is a beach girl.

We each take an end of the blanket and spread it out right at the edge of the beach, as close to her house as we can get without leaving the sand. I sit down first, then pull her to sit between my legs, leaning her back against my chest. We both stare out at the water, it appears black in the light of the moon. Almost dangerous.

I trace my hands up and down her arms, loving the way she shivers at the contact. She always reacts to my touch...she can't hide a thing. Not from me. She rests her head on my right shoulder, and turns her head so she's looking up at me. I look down at her and the look in her eyes makes my breath catch.

She wants me.

Her ocean blue eyes are filled with pure lust.

Without wasting another minute, I lean down and capture her lips with mine. I twist my body, gently pressing her down onto the blanket and moving myself to hover above her. I'm careful not to press all my weight against her, using one arm to hold myself up while the other softly grazes her smooth thigh, moving up below her dress until I determine that she is indeed wearing panties under that dress.

She squirms beneath me in an obvious attempt to get my hand where she wants it...right at the hot spot between her legs. I move my hand closer, then pull back from her lips to look into her eyes.

Is this what she really wants?

"Please," she confirms as she grinds herself into me.

I groan and take her lips again, my hand finally finding its way into her slick, wet heat. I rub, stroke, flick, and curl my fingers against her until she's screaming my name right there on the sand.

She wraps her arms around my shoulders and kisses me deeply. Like she can't get enough. I realize, when she whispers "more" into my mouth, that she truly can't get enough.

Neither can I.

Chapter Thirty

Sara

I give Trevor the green light, and he strips us both of our clothes, sheathes himself, and thrusts inside of me before I can even blink. I moan at the welcome intrusion and firmly wrap my legs around his waist. My hands are everywhere as he pistons in and out. I can't get enough of his defined arms, rippling abs, and firm ass. His left arm still holds his body securely above mine so as not to crush me, while his other hand explores every inch of me he can reach. Our mouths are fused together, separating only to lick and suck the nearest pleasure zone. Then he flips us over, and I start riding him. I think I might burst from the new angle.

Whatever *this* is between Trevor and me...it is nothing I've ever experienced before. After riding him for only a few minutes—circling and grinding against his pelvis in an oh-so-delicious rhythm—we both come, screaming into the night. I collapse on top of him.

I eventually roll off of him, and he pulls me into his side. We both lie on the blanket, staring into the starry night. Lost in our own thoughts, I assume. I hadn't exactly been abstinent since Lucas, but I didn't get around much either. Just a few partners here and there. I just didn't have the time. This unlike anything else...ever.

He reaches over, grasps my hand, and I smile into the night.

"That was...amazing," he says quietly, sounding awestruck.

"It was," I agree. I'm about to suggest we go at it again when he says something that has me sitting straight up.

"Want to go check on the kids?"

The kids! Ohmygod!

I scramble around the blanket, looking for my dress and panties, and quickly pull them on.

"What's wrong?" Trevor asks, taking the hint and getting dressed himself.

"I can't believe I did this. So irresponsible. Having sex on the beach while the kids are inside asleep. What if something happened? What if they came out here? What if they *heard* us?" I stand up and start yanking on the blanket, almost causing Trevor to fall as he was still standing on it.

"Hey. Sara," he grabs my hand. "Stop it for a minute, will you?" He lifts my chin and looks into my eyes, my light to his dark. "You said it yourself, they sleep deeply after they go down, and they would have flashed the light if they woke up."

"But I wasn't paying attention, Trevor! They could have flashed the light, and I didn't see it."

"They didn't."

"How the hell do you know?" I bark at him, yanking back my hand and roughly folding up the blanket I'm still holding.

"Because I was looking. I had my eye on the house the whole time, I swear. Just calm down."

"I'm not going to calm down," I tell him before storming away towards the house. I hear his footsteps behind me and get angry all over again.

Here I am, having to fight for custody of these kids—kids I've practically raised since they were born—and I leave them alone in the house—at night—while I have a romp on the beach. Real fucking responsible, Miss Sands. That'll look great in court. What if Nora has someone watching the house? What if she's hired a private detective to follow me around? The thought has me pause in my steps, and Trevor bumps into my back, immediately placing his hands on my shoulders to steady me. I shrug out his grip and shake the terrifying thoughts away as I jog the last few spaces to the steps and run up them and inside.

It's not until I'm standing outside the twins' rooms, looking in at their precious, undisturbed, sleeping faces, that I relax. I feel Trevor's presence behind me and sink back into it as he wraps his arms possessively around my shoulders. I don't deserve this beautiful, wonderful man. But I've got him. At least for the next couple weeks.

"I'm so sorry," I whisper.

"Want to tell me what that was about?" he says back, just as softly.

"I'm scared," I confess. "I'm so scared that I'll make one wrong move and all this will be gone." I sniffle, and it's then I realize I'm crying.

Trevor turns me into his chest and puts his arms around my shoulders, pulling me in close. "Shh," he says while gently stroking my back. "You're not going to lose those kids," he says with a conviction he can't possibly mean. He doesn't know what's going to happen at court.

"You don't know that."

"I know that you are the best possible person for those kids to be with. You love them fiercely and unconditionally. The court may not see that right away, but they *will* see it."

I want to believe him so badly. He sounds so certain, as if he's got some kind of inside scoop. I know that's not possible, though.

"Come on," he says, tugging me towards the stairs. "There's some ice cream in the freezer we didn't finish earlier."

I softly giggle as he leads me down the stairs. I love how he can turn my mood around. The fear is still present, but it's subdued. "You really know the way to a woman's heart," I joke.

He looks over his shoulder at me and winks. I melt a little bit. When we get downstairs, he deposits me on the couch with the remote and heads off to the kitchen. After spending the day here, he sure has made himself at home. I smile at the thought of him really making himself at home here, then frown. Too bad it could never be.

He returns with a tub of ice cream neatly wrapped in a kitchen towel and a spoon. I plaster on my fake smile and take the offered items, thanking him with a kiss on the cheek. He's got a slight stubble going, and it tickles my lips. I'd like to run my tongue along his jawline, nibbling slightly before I reach his earlobe and—

"Whatcha thinking about?" he asks with a Cheshire cat grin. His laughing eyes tell me he knows exactly what station my train of thought derailed at.

I shrug my shoulders and dig into the ice cream. "Want some?" I ask him after my fifth consecutive spoonful.

"I thought you'd never ask," he growls, taking the spoon from my hand and digging in. He eats a few bites, then catches me staring at his mouth and sets the container down on the coffee table. My cheeks heat as he turns his devilish stare on me.

"You'd better behave," I warn. "The kids are—"

"Asleep," he says, just before he takes my mouth in a bruising kiss, and I'm grateful that my earlier hissy fit didn't send him running for the hills.

We don't have sex. We don't even get naked. But we do roll around on the couch making out like teenagers for an hour before Trevor gets a text from Chase asking if he still needs to be picked up. Part of me wants him to stay, but I know it's best for the kids if he doesn't. It's probably best for my heart as well. If I were to wake up in my bed next to Trevor, there would be no going back.

At midnight, Trevor kisses me goodbye on my front step. Our hands remain linked until he steps too far away, and our eyes stay connected until Chase pulls the van out of the driveway and onto the street.

It's then that I realize...it may already be too late for my heart.

Chapter Thirty-One

Trevor

Two more weeks. Two weeks. Fourteen days. Three hundred and thirty-six hours. Twenty thousand some odd minutes. A whole lot of seconds.

Still not enough time.

I saw Sara again last night. Couldn't seem to stay away. I snuck over in the van after everyone in both houses were asleep. Everyone except for me and her. Being with her a second time was just as good, if not better, than the first time. Last night, we took it slow, and I got to roam over every last inch of her delicate, decadent body.

"Are you even paying attention?" Chase asks with an annoyed tone causing Sara to giggle.

Yeah, she's here right now, cuddled up on the couch with me while the guys and I have an impromptu band meeting. She stopped by on her way to work, after dropping off the kids, and I haven't let her leave. After kissing her at the door for several minutes, I ignored her protests and pulled her into the second floor living room where the rest of the guys were seated. Initially, she froze in place at the sudden audience, obviously feeling awkward, but I just tugged her down beside me on the couch and firmly held her in place until she relaxed into my side.

For the past several minutes, I've been absently running my fingers through my hair and replaying the last two nights together in my mind. Hence Chase's orneriness. Hell, can't say I blame him because if it was any of them, I would have been the one pissed.

"Give him a break," Alex says. "He's finally getting some."

I reach over and pop my brother in the back of the head.

"I should go," Sara says, sitting up. I don't need to see her face to know she's blushing.

"No," I grunt, just like a caveman, and pull her back into my side.

"I'm distracting you," she protests. I ignore her. "Plus, this is band business, and I'm not in the band. The other girls aren't here."

"Shh," I tell her and nod at Chase to go on. He shakes his head, but he's smiling. It's been a while since he's seen me with a woman like this—if ever.

"So we have to hit the studio a week or so after we get home." I barely feel Sara tense under my arm, but it happens. I know she doesn't like to be reminded that this isn't my home, but it's the reality we have to live with. I squeeze her leg, hoping to relax her. It works, and I feel her body relax. "We'll have a couple weeks to practice, if we need it, then Trevor and Joe are up. And Alex and I will finish it off. Recording the album itself shouldn't take that long. As usual, we're ahead of schedule so we can kind of take our time with it."

"Why do I always have to go last?" Alex whines. I don't know why he always complains about going last. Lead vocals and lead guitar are always last. Bass and drums go first. It's not our first time in the studio, and the order is nothing new.

I ignore him and look at Chase. "What else?"

Chase's eyes dart from mine to Sara's, then back to mine. "The tour starts in November."

"This is gonna be awesome. Max is gonna love the new bus," Joey says.

"You're taking Max on tour?" Sara asks him.

Joey gives her an odd look. "Of course...can't exactly leave him home by himself."

"Evie goes, too?"

Joey nods and grins. "She's the official band photographer. She takes pictures to put on the website and Facebook and stuff. This will be Max's first full tour. Our last bus was kind of small, hard to have a kid on board."

"Yeah, he's got a lot of shit," Alex adds.

"Don't call my kid's stuff 'shit,'" Joey says, punching Alex in the arm.

"Ouch! What is with all this physical violence towards me?" Alex whines, rubbing his arm.

"Maybe if you'd think before you spoke you wouldn't get hit," Chase tells him.

"I don't have to take this abuse," Alex says, then he turns his puppy dog eyes to Sara. "Sara, will you come rub my arm for me? Kiss it and make it feel better?"

I move to stand up, and this time it's Sara who is holding me down...while shaking in laughter. "Oh, you think that's funny?"

She looks up at me, her blue eyes sparkling. "Yes, I think it's hilarious the way you all pick at each other." I'm about to flip her over and tickle her mercilessly, but the sudden shift in her eyes stops me cold. Her usually bright blue eyes are suddenly dull.

"Are you okay?" I ask, smoothing my thumb over her cheek.

She seems to snap out of whatever place she was in and gives me a fake smile. "I'm fine. Just thinking about all the stuff waiting for me at work."

"Liar," I tell her, but I leave it alone. For now. I lean back into the cushions, still holding her, as we listen to Chase go on about the different cities we'll be visiting this tour. This one will go through mostly southern states since it'll cross into the winter. Buses and snow aren't a fun combination. Next we talk about what old songs to pull off the set lists to make room for the new stuff. I smile every once in a while when Sara pipes in that she likes a particular song, and we shouldn't take it off the list.

This very moment, I can picture what my life might be like with Sara in it. Beyond today, beyond this month, and beyond the Outer Banks.

***

I somehow managed to talk Sara out of going to work today. I know, I'm a terrible influence, and I did feel a little guilty about it...but only a little. Sitting on the couch with her, lounging around and talking to my brothers, it felt right and comfortable, and I didn't want it to end. Sue me. Ally and Evie came down after Max went down for his nap, and they both smiled when they saw Sara. We all ended up sitting in the second floor living room for hours, talking about nothing and everything. It felt right. Perfect.

Now, I'm walking Sara out to her car so she can go pick up the kids from day camp.

"I had a really great time today," I tell her as I hold her close. Her head rests just below my chin. It's a perfect fit. We're a perfect fit.

"Me, too," she says. I don't have to be looking at her to know that her eyes are closed, and she's absorbing every moment, just like me.

"You freaked me out a little bit earlier, and I know you weren't thinking about work. Wanna talk about it?"

I feel her take a deep breath against my chest. "It's just me being silly is all."

"Hey...if you're thinking it or feeling it, then it's not silly."

"I was just having fun with y'all. You're a real family. I never really had that. I mean, my parents were great; they were good parents, but I didn't have any kind of sibling fun or anything like that. And everything in my house was pretty formal. It just kind of hit me all at once, you know? I want Georgie and Gwen to have something like that growing up. I want them to have what I didn't."

I swallow past the lump in my throat. My poor girl. She has so much love and affection to give, and it's been bottled up until the past few years when she could share it with the twins and now—hopefully—with me.

"You can still have that," I tell her, rubbing her back. "You can be an honorary member of our family." I stiffen, realizing how that sounds. "Uh...like how Evie is a member of our family?" Well that's not much better since Joey and Evie are *married*. "Um..." I feel Sara's body shaking in my arms and pull away, thinking she's crying. "You're laughing?"

She nods. "It's hilarious when you trip over yourself like that. You're like Superman, you know? You're strong and stoic, like all the time, so when you do something goofy, like trip over your words, it makes me laugh. Reminds me that you're human, too."

"You think I'm like Superman?" I ask with a smirk, feeling pretty good about myself.

She rolls her eyes. "Of course, that's all you'd pick up on. Yes, I think you're like superman. You'd save the world if you could."

"Yeah, I would," I agree. "You know what's great about being a superhero?" Sara closes her eyes, and I hear her mumbling to herself about how she shouldn't have said anything and something about my ego being big enough as it is. I laugh and say, "My ego isn't all that's big."

She smacks my arm and laughs. "You're a mess."

I want to tell her that I'll be "her mess" as long as she lets me, but I don't. Instead, I grab onto her waist and pull her against me. "You didn't answer me."

"What?"

"Do you know what's great about being a superhero?"

She sighs, but plays along. "What's so great about being a superhero?"

"Superheroes get to kiss the girl," I say, then lean down to do just that. Her arms snake around my neck and mine around her waist. I love the feel of her body so tight against mine. I wish we could stay like this forever, but she pulls away.

"You're a cheeseball," she tells me. "I have to go get the kids. I'm gonna be late."

"Okay. Drive safe," I tell her as she hops in her Jeep. "I'll talk to you later."

She smiles and leans out to give me one last peck before she shuts the door. "See ya later."

I watch her pull out of the driveway and onto the road, my eyes not leaving the road until they can no longer see her. I rub my chest. It physically hurts to be without her. Today was amazing. A glimpse at what life could be like if we made it past this month.

I want that. I want *her*.

Now all that's left is figuring out what to do about it.

Chapter Thirty-Two

Sara

Work's been busy with training new staff, and Gwen's been dealing with a summer cold, so I haven't seen Trevor since our impromptu visit on Tuesday when I spent the day with him and the band. I've been passing out exhausted around ten o'clock, so our late night trysts have been non-existent as well.

I *miss* him.

I *want* him.

Tonight, I'm gonna have him.

When I spoke with him via text this morning, I told him Gwen still wasn't feeling well, so it wasn't likely we'd be able to get together today.

I lied.

Gwen is feeling much, much better. Through a group text with Ally and Evie this morning, I arranged for the twins to have a sleepover with Max. Ally is going to take Trevor to my house later under the guise of bringing Gwen some soup. Then she's going to leave with the kids. Gwen and Georgie are excited. They've been chattering about the pool and the movie room ever since I picked them up from day camp and told them their plans for the night.

It's almost six, they should be here any minute!

I holler up the stairs for Georgie and Gwen to bring their bags down for inspection. I generally let them pack their own bags when we go out, but I reserve the right to replace any mismatching or audacious items. Once, Gwen tried to slip her bunny slippers passed me for a trip to the beach. It would have taken me forever to get the sand out of that faux fur.

I hear the stampede on the wooden stairs and shake my head as I wait. Whoever coined the term "pitter-patter of little feet" must not have had kids. Or hardwood floors.

"Let me see what you've got." Gwen proudly holds out her bag, and I take a peek, feeling around for any odd items. She's got matching clothes for tomorrow and pajamas for tonight, a couple picture books, and one doll. Her travel toothbrush is in the outside pocket. I nod and give her a smile, letting her know she did well.

Georgie reluctantly holds out his bag, and it makes me a little nervous since he'd once packed a lizard. I resist the temptation of dumping his bag on the ground and give him the benefit of the doubt. I look at his clothes and see all necessary items are accounted for. He also has a couple books, a GI Joe doll, and a few toy cars. I smile at another job well done, then raise my eyebrows when I notice his toothbrush is missing. He sighs, knowing he's been caught, and runs up the stairs, returning a minute later with the toothbrush. The kid hates brushing his teeth!

"Good job, guys."

"I'm not a guy; I'm a girl," Gwen says.

"You're right. I should've said, 'good job, guy and girl.'"

Gwen laughs. "You're so silly, Auntie."

"Why don't you choose a movie to bring over?"

"Auntie, they have *billions* of movies!" Georgie tells me.

"Oh, I hadn't realized." Just then, I hear the sound of tires on the gravel drive and the twins shriek with excitement. "Get your bags! Georgie, did you want to bring Teddy?" I ask, referring to the stuffed bear he takes with him everywhere.

"Auntie, I'm a big boy now," he says as he brings his bag to the front door and opens it wide. "They're here!"

Both kids go running out the front door and down the steps, bags in tow. Wow. Not even a goodbye. No Teddy? They're only six. They can't be growing up that fast. I swallow the lump in my throat, the one that always seems to make an appearance when I realize they're not babies anymore and are turning into quite the little independent humans.

"Why do I have the feeling I've been had?"

Having zoned out for a moment, I jump at the sound of Trevor's voice. I smile as he climbs the steps and lean into his chest, loving the instant pick-me-up I feel when he wraps his strong arms around me.

"Sorry," I say, not actually sorry at all.

"You can fool me anytime you want if the end result is us getting to spend some time alone."

I smile against his chest, then lean back. "Surprise."

"Incoming," Ally calls as she walks in the front door with the twins trailing behind her. She's got that same basket with her that Trevor had with him last weekend.

"Soup?" I ask. I know it was all a ruse, but she didn't have to follow through with making the soup.

"Just some treats," she chirps, winking at me before turning to the kids. "Are you both ready to go have some fun?"

"Yeah!" the kids shout.

"Say goodnight, and we'll go."

Both kids come running over and tackle my legs.

"Night, Auntie," Gwen says.

"Night," Georgie says, his voice muffled by my dress.

"You two have fun. Call me if you want to talk, okay?" They both nod, but who am I kidding? They won't call. They haven't been this excited in ages. They're going to wear themselves out and pass out nice and early. I don't even feel bad for sending them off with Ally.

Gwen shyly says goodbye to Trevor before following Ally to the door, but Georgie stays behind. I squat down to his level. "What's up, bud?" He looks at me timidly, twisting his hands in front of him—a habit he undoubtedly picked up from me. "You can stay home if you want to, you know that, don't you?"

His eyes widen. "No, I wanna go."

"Then what's up?"

He leans in close and whispers, "I think I wanna bring Teddy."

I smile. My sweet boy. Of course, he does. I blink back the emotion from my eyes. "Where's your bag?" I ask quietly, realizing he wants to keep Teddy on the down low.

"In the car already," he frowns.

"Okay, Georgie," I say, standing back up. "You can bring your pillow." He looks at me oddly, but I turn to his sister. "Gwen, do you want yours as well?"

"Uh huh," she answers before returning to her excited chatter with Ally about who knows what.

"I'll be right back." I run upstairs and get Gwen's pillow from her bedroom, then head into Georgie's room. I get his pillow and Teddy and stuff Teddy inside the pillowcase. When I hand him the pillow downstairs, it takes him a minute to realize there's a stowaway, but when he does, his eyes brighten up and he runs into my legs again.

"Thank you, Auntie."

"You're welcome, Georgie. Go! Have fun!" I pat him on his butt, and he runs for the door. I mouth "Thank you" to Ally, and she smiles and winks in response.

When the door shuts behind them, I finally turn towards Trevor, who has been quietly leaning against the kitchen doorframe. Butterflies flutter in my tummy. I have no idea why I'm feeling nervous. It's not like I've never been alone with Trevor before. Maybe it's because this is the first time we're really, truly alone. No interruptions. No kids to distract me. The night is completely ours.

"So, Mr. Monroe," I say with a flirty smile as I strut over to him, swaying my hips seductively as I move. "What do you want to do?"

Chapter Thirty-Three

Trevor

"Would it be terribly boring of me to say that I want to take you out?" Sara is a vision. Even more so now since it's been a couple days since I last saw her. She can wear absolutely anything, but when she's in blue...it makes her eyes pop...and she has the most beautiful eyes I've ever seen. The sundress she's wearing is the same pale blue as the one she wore our first time, bringing back lots of naughty memories, but it's got little sleeves that touch the tips of her shoulders while the other one had straps. I can't tell if she's wearing a bra with this one.

She looks surprised at my question, then relaxes her expression. "Of course, it wouldn't be boring," she smiles.

"It's just that we never get the chance to actually go out and I thought—"

She places her hand on my arm. "Trevor, it's okay. I'd love to go out. I just wasn't sure you'd want to chance being seen."

I rub the back of my neck and give her a sheepish smile. "I hadn't thought of that."

"It's not a big deal. We can just hang out here. I can order takeout. But first, let's see what Ally packed us," she slips by me and into the kitchen.

I can't believe they plotted this behind my back. Actually, yes...yes, I can believe it. This scheme has Ally written all over it. All Sara would have had to do is plant the seed and my sister would have come up with a big elaborate plan. It's just one of the many characteristics of Ally that have been returning after her amnesia, and I'm not complaining one bit. I love having my sister back, and I love that my sister and my girl get along.

I sigh. Not *my* girl.

"What's wrong?" Sara asks as she lifts the hinged lid of the basket.

"Nothing," I say, smiling to reassure her. "I just can't believe you pulled this off."

She smirks. "I didn't like lying to you this morning, but it was fun. I've been excited all day."

"Oh yeah?" I grin and waggle my eyebrows. "How excited?"

Her cheeks pink. "You're so bad. Not *that* kind of excited. Yet." I walk up behind her and put my hands on her hips as she digs through the basket. "Your sister has a naughty streak," she says, and I resist the temptation to put my hands over my ears and go, "la la la la la."

Instead I ask, "What's in there?"

Sara starts pulling items out and setting them on the countertop. Champagne. Strawberries. Whipped cream. Chocolate sauce. Honey. *Honey?*

"Jeez, did she include any soap? That's bound to get messy." The next two things Sara pulls out are an aromatherapy candle and matching bubble bath, both labeled "sensual." I involuntarily shiver when I think about my little sister packing this stuff for me.

"She thought of everything," Sara laughs. "Why don't we take a look at some takeout menus before we start getting hungry for dessert?" She winks, and I'm already hard. I groan as she brushes against me, leaning across the counter to grab a few menus she must have already pulled out. Her sweet, round ass is right there in front of me, and I want to grab it, squeeze it, lick it, bite it...and if she doesn't stop teasing me, spank it.

She fans out the menus in front of me. "What are you in the mood for?" None of them say "Sara," so I shrug and point to one. I don't even know which one. "Ooh," she squeals. I wasn't aware that Sara squealed. "This is my favorite sushi place. Just wait until you try their volcano roll. It's to die for."

She rambles on and on about every delicious sushi roll on the menu and all I can think about is what I'm going to do to her later. Whipped cream and chocolate have never looked so good.

***

"What's the farthest city you've visited on tour?" Sara asks me later that evening while we're soaking in her oversized tub with the sensual bubble bath, lit only by the light of the sensual candle. Not really sure what's so *sensual* about it all.

"Vancouver, maybe? Not really sure of the mileage." Underwater, I run my hands up her slippery legs to her tummy, her skin slick from the bubble bath. I love the way my hands slide across her smooth skin, though I kind of miss the hot, stickiness of all the sweets I licked off of her just an hour before.

"Washington? Or Canada?"

"Canada."

"Ooh, you're an international rock star," she teases with a giggle. A giggle that turns into a whimper when I pinch her nipple.

"Still want to tease me?"

"I'll behave," she says breathlessly, tipping her head back on my shoulder as my right hand caresses her breast and my left hand moves between her legs.

"Where's the fun in that?" I whisper as I nip her earlobe.

"You don't play fair," she pants.

She rocks herself against my hand, which in turn is grinding her ass against my length. I thrust against her backside and she lets out a satisfying moan. Her breaths quicken, and I feel her tightening around my fingers. I give her breast one last squeeze, and she shatters in my arms. Once she stops trembling, she relaxes against me, her body boneless.

"I beg to differ. I think that was very, very fair."

She twists in my arms so that she's straddling my waist. I send a silent prayer of thanks to whoever picked out this bathtub. It's just large enough that we can both fit, while still being cozy. I feel her center press against my length and I freeze, wanting so badly to just slip inside...but I don't have a condom in here with me—*stupid*—and Sara and I haven't had the alternative-

contraception-slash-safe-sex   talk   yet—
stupider.

She gives me a long, sensual—*thank you, candles and bubbles!*—kiss, making love to my mouth with hers. My hands immediately go to her ass, and I squeeze the small, round globes. But before I can pull her close, she pulls back.

"Uh uh," she says, wagging her finger in front of my face. I have half a mind to bite it, the tease. "Sit up top," she gestures to the tile ledge surrounding the tub. I comply, not really sure where this is heading, but eager as hell to find out.

With a saucy little smirk on her face, Sara crawls to me through the water, on her knees, causing my dick to twitch—to be honest, the sight of Sara on her knees, naked and wet, has me about to blow...I'm lucky all it did was twitch.

She nestles herself right between my legs and runs her hands up my legs, bracing them on my thighs. I reach forward to take her by the waist and haul her ass into my lap, but she leans back and "tsk tsks" me. I'm about to argue when her small hand grips my shaft, and she licks me from root to tip. I lean back against the cool tile wall behind me and groan.

Sara sucks and licks and strokes and nips until a flurry of incoherencies fly out of my mouth. I grip her hair and try to pull her off, letting her know I'm about to come but she only sucks harder. She looks up at me, determination in her eyes, and that's it. I buck and crash into a million pieces.

Holy shit.

Chapter Thirty-Four

Sara

The morning sunlight and sea breeze enter my room through the open French doors of my balcony. I point my toes and stretch my arms above my head, smiling at how deliciously sore I am from last night's activities. I roll to my side and lean my head in my hand, staring down at the handsome man beside me. His dark eyelashes just touch the tops of his cheeks and a small smile is on his face. He looks so peaceful in his sleep.

I get up to use the bathroom and brush my teeth. He still hasn't woken up when I come out, and since I don't have the kids, I opt to slide back under the covers with him. I love the way his naked body feels pressed up against mine. I press myself against his side and lift my leg across his, feeling kind of frisky and hoping it'll wake him up.

It doesn't.

Frowning, I consider poking him until he wakes up. But then I have a better idea. I slide my body over his, not gracefully at all, until I'm hovering right over top of him, and touch my slick center to his raging morning wood.

Suddenly, his hands are on my ass and he pulls me down as he thrusts up. His erection rubs against me and leaves me squirming in the most delicious way.

"What a way to wake up," he says, his voice raspy with sleep.

"Mm, you sound sexy in the morning."

He smirks, his eyes still closed. "Do I?"

"Mm hmm." I rub my nose against his, licking his lips.

"Is that why you're trying to take advantage of me?"

"I was trying to do that before you even woke up," I tell him.

"Naughty girl," he says as he rolls us over so he's on top.

I tilt my head up and nip at his bottom lip. "I want you so bad," I tell him with a pout. I'm not sure what's gotten into me. I went without sex for a while before Trevor, now I'm practically insatiable.

He smiles before taking my mouth in a kiss I'd call panty-melting, if I was wearing panties. He reaches over to the nightstand for a condom, rolls it on, and pushes inside of me, never once removing his lips from mine. His tongue thrusts in time with his hips, and it doesn't take long before we're coming apart in each other's arms. Again.

***

"I could get used to this," Trevor says as we eat our breakfast on the beach. I look at him, trying to gauge the seriousness of his statement. Is he just saying that to make conversation? Or could he really get used to this? Does he *want* to get used to it?

Stop thinking so hard, Sara! You're reading way too far into something that was probably just casually said. He has a life back in Charlotte. He's going in the studio and then on tour. He's not going to live here with you.

"It's too bad we missed sunrise."

"Eh, we can see those any day of the week. It's not every day I get to wake up next to the most beautiful girl in the world." He smiles at me, and I'm putty.

Why does this have to end?

"So court's Monday. Wanna talk about it?"

I frown. "Not particularly, no. Maybe later." I don't want to taint this day with talk about Nora. There's nothing I can do at this point anyway but show up at court and wait.

"When is Ally dropping the kids off?" he asks, lying back on the blanket and rolling to his side to face me. Ah, safe topic.

"Later this afternoon. She said she'd call if she thought they needed a break from each other earlier than that."

"So we've still got some alone time, eh?" he smiles mischievously and pulls me down beside him.

"Yes, but we are on a public beach."

"Hasn't stopped us before," he says, kissing my neck and sliding his hand under my shirt.

"Yeah, well, it's daylight and I have neighbors." A dog barks somewhere nearby, punctuating my statement. I raise my eyebrow. "See?"

"This has been one of the best times I've ever had in my life," he tells me and my eyes instantly fill with tears. It's like he's already saying goodbye. Planting a little reminder that this is just a *time* in his life. It's not his life.

"Me, too," I tell him, offering a small smile. I roll over and lift myself up, resting on my elbows. If I keep looking into his eyes, I might break. I'll save that for later today...once he's gone and the kids are in bed.

He mimics my pose and watches as I draw my hearts in the sand. Then, for every heart I draw, he draws one intertwined with mine. My pulse races along with my mind as I think about what his actions mean.

Is his heart involved?

He can't possibly love me...it's too soon for that. But does he want more? He implied he'd be interested in seeing where this went, if it came down to it.

Is that what this is? More?

I shake off those thoughts and go with a safe topic. "What other tourist activities do y'all have planned?"

"Well, Miss Sands, Tour Guide Extraordinaire, what do you suggest?" He smiles when I giggle at his silliness, both of us still absently drawing hearts.

We've nearly filled this edge of the blanket, so I wipe the slate clean and start over again. "Well, Mr. Monroe...you've done a horse tour, played mini-golf, rented jet skis and ATVs, and visited the Wright Brothers Memorial. Did I miss anything?"

"You forgot parasailing, but that about sums it up."

"There are some aquariums. Max would probably like that. And places to bird watch and fish. Nature preserves..." I trail off when I catch him staring at me. "What? Do I have something on my face?" I wipe my cheeks and chin, getting sand on them in the process.

"No," he says simply. "I was just thinking that I'd rather spend the rest of my time here with you than do anything else. You're the only thing I want to see and explore."

My heart stutters in my chest. I almost swoon from his words, but it could just be the heat. "You shouldn't say things like that."

"Why not?"

"Because this is temporary. You leave in ten days."

He lets out a frustrated sigh and rolls onto his back. "But who's counting?"

I chew on my lip. He obviously doesn't appreciate the reminder of our deadline. But what can I do? I can't delude myself into believing this can be a long term thing. I'm already feeling *way* too much for this man. It's self-preservation at its finest. Reminding myself that the end is near is how I check myself with a small dose of reality. It's not working so well since I'm crazy about him anyway, but it's worth a shot...right?

"I'm gonna go for a swim," he says as he quickly stands up. Before I can even respond—let alone get up to join him—he's racing down to the water.

I watch his retreating form and remind myself that this is what it's going to be like in ten days when he leaves. It'll be me watching as he walks away.

Me getting left behind...again.

Chapter Thirty-Five

Trevor

I'm pacing around the room, waiting to hear from Sara. Since pacing has become my norm on this trip, and my family seems to love to pick on me about it, I'm hiding away in my bedroom. Makes the pacing kind of hard since I have an enormous bed to contend with, but I'm managing.

Court started two hours ago, and I'm antsy as hell. I wish she would have let me be there to support her, even just by waiting in the lobby or something, but she'd turned me down flat when I asked. Ever since the beach on Saturday, we've both been a little distant. I think the reality that this—whatever *this* is— will soon be ending is hitting us both. The difference now versus a week ago is that now we have feelings for each other. She doesn't have to tell me, I can see it in her eyes. Just like I'm sure she can see it in mine. I held on to her so tight when my sister came to pick me up. I didn't want to let go. I'd still be holding her if I had the choice.

I just wish there was a way to break through the fortress she's built around herself. I know she's been burned before, and I know our situation is far from the norm, but I feel like we're giving up before we even get the chance to try. And I am not a quitter. It goes against my nature to not fight for what I want...what I believe in...what I care about. And I want her, I believe in her, and I care about her.

Finally, at half past eleven, she calls me.

Sitting down on the edge of my bed, I accept the call. "Hey, pretty girl. How did it go?" She sniffles. That's not a good sign. *Fuck!* "I'm sorry, babe."

She lets out a sigh. "It wasn't terrible, but it wasn't good either. They're giving her a chance," she says, sounding disgusted. I can't blame her; I'm disgusted myself, and I wasn't even there.

"What does that mean?" I ask.

"It means she'll be given supervised visitations. There will be a social worker involved. It's just like Mr. Adelson said. One strike and she's out. But she's already had a court-approved social worker do a home study and she passed with flying colors. It's how she was even able to petition for custody in the first place. Apparently she has a steady job and has been living with her *fiancé* for more than a year now. He was there."

"But what about that incident at your house?" I ask, referring to when Nora had gotten pissed and did donuts in her driveway before leaving.

She huffs. "They excused it as her being emotional because I was keeping her from her kids. That she just wanted to see her kids and my keeping her from them made her upset. She apologized for reacting in an immature way and everyone fell for it."

"I'm so sorry, Sara."

"Don't be, it's not your fault."

"I know it's not. I'm just sorry it didn't turn out better. But like you said, one strike and she's out. Just keep an eagle eye on her. And hey, maybe this will be a good thing? Maybe she really is trying to turn over a new leaf."

"I hate that saying."

I laugh. "Me, too. My mom always used to say it, though. It stuck."

"I don't think she's trying to do good here, Trevor. I would love to believe that, to have hope—for the sake of the kids—but the way she looked at me when she walked out of the courtroom…it was so cold. I don't expect any kind of award for taking care of the twins the past four years, but she didn't even acknowledge what I've done for them—for her. If I were her and I was trying to make things better, I would at least show some appreciation towards the person who has been keeping them alive and well all this time. How can the court overlook things like that?"

"I wish I knew." I wish there was something I could do to make this better—hell, to make it all disappear—but I've got nothing. Nothing short of a miracle will make this better for Sara and the twins.

"I'm really sorry, Trevor, but I'm gonna need a few days. I know we don't have much time left, but I need to deal with this. Mentally, I'm a mess. And I have to prepare the kids. I just can't be worrying about one more thing right now."

I'm a little stunned—and annoyed, if I'm being honest—that I've been added to a list of her worries and just as easily dismissed, but I can't exactly blame her either. I knew if the outcome was poor, she'd need time. So time is what I'll give her.

"It's okay, do what you need to do. I'd like to be there for you, whenever you're ready for me to be. I don't want you going through all this alone."

"I appreciate that. I really do. And I might take you up on it. But right now I've got to focus on Georgie and Gwen and make sure they're okay. The first visit is in two weeks."

"So soon?"

She scoffs. "Yeah. She passed with flying colors, remember?"

"That's such crap."

"Tell me about it."

"I know you just said you needed time, but I want to hold you right now. Badly."

"I want that, too. More than anything," she says quietly.

"Where are you?"

"At home. I'd be completely useless at the office today. I have to pick up the kids in a few hours."

"Can I come over?" I ask, jumping from the bed and grabbing my wallet and aviators off the side table. I suppose I should wait for her to say yes, but I'm not sure I'm really giving her an option here.

"I don't know, Trevor."

"Just for a minute. Just to hold you. You're so strong, Sara. You take care of every*one* and every*thing* around you as best you can. You need someone to take care of you for a minute. Let me take care of you."

"Okay," she agrees.

"Really?" I'd expected a little more of a fight.

"Yeah, come over," she says softly, and I hear the smile in her voice.

"I'll be right there." I hang up the phone and run up the steps to get the keys off the counter. I tell Chase—who is on the couch with yet another biography—that I'm taking the van and I'll be back in a few. He nods without looking up from his book. The rest of the family went down to the beach thirty minutes ago, so I know no one needs to go anywhere in the next hour or so.

I probably break at least six traffic laws on my way to Sara's house, but she's granted me a small window, and I want it to start as soon as possible. I park in her driveway a few minutes later and jog up the front steps to the house. I'm panting when she opens the door.

"Are you okay?" she asks with an eyebrow raised.

"Need...more...cardio," I say between inhales.

"Did you run here?" she asks, looking around me to the driveway.

I shake my head. "Just up the driveway and steps."

"You're out of shape," she says pointedly.

I stand up straight. *What?* "I'll show you out of shape," I say, ripping my t-shirt over my head and pushing her into the house, letting the front door slam behind us.

"Oh, yes...show me."

Chapter Thirty-Six

Sara

Trevor gave me two full days to deal with my stuff before he came banging my door down. I appreciate his tenacity, I just wish he was a local.

Today is Thursday, and he leaves on Monday. Five days.

The sun is shining a soft pink glow across the sky while waves lap at the shore. It's a picturesque summer evening. The twins are a few paces ahead, collecting rocks and shells and who knows what else in their little pails. Trevor and I are strolling behind them, hand in hand. Like I said, picturesque.

I told myself not to do this tonight, but I can't help it. It's been weighing so heavily on my mind the past two days. When my thoughts weren't with the twins, they were with Trevor.

Five more days. Just enjoy the next five days, Sara!

"What do you want to happen here?" I mentally smack myself in the forehead. Open mouth and insert foot.

Trevor looks over at me, seeming a little lost. I can't imagine why he might feel lost, seeing as I just pulled that question out of thin air and all.

"With us, I mean. Where do you see this going?" I clarify.

"Do you see us going somewhere?" he asks. I look at him again, and my heart hurts a little when I see the hopeful sparkle in his eyes.

"I asked you first." Facepalm. Again. He smirks at my silliness. I'm not even trying to be funny, but I'm glad he thinks it's amusing. Maybe that'll make this easier. Or worse. One or the other.

"Well, I'd like to see you beyond this month, Sara. I'd love to." He squeezes the hand he's holding, and I stare at where we're joined as we walk.

"How?"

"What?"

"How would we see each other after this month?"

"You could come visit me. Or I could visit you," he quickly adds when he sees my eyes narrow.

"But we can't just keep doing that. The back and forth. I can't be away from the kids for days at a time and I can't exactly bring them with me, either. Who knows what's going to happen with Nora, and I probably won't be able to do much traveling at all because of that mess."

"Hey, we can figure it out. Go with the flow. You can come stay with me in the off-season maybe."

I yank my hand away. "Stay with you in the off-season? Are you crazy? There is no off-season with kids. They have a life here, Trevor. I have a life here."

He sighs, stops walking, and turns to face me. "Then what do you suggest?"

"I don't know."

"Well, I have a life in Charlotte, too. I'm trying to compromise—"

"But you're not compromising. You're telling me I should move to Charlotte in the non-existent off-season."

He runs his hand through his hair, then rubs the back of his neck. "Why are we fighting?"

"We're not fighting."

"Yeah, we are. We were walking, things were nice, and then you attacked me."

"I attacked you?" The nerve!

"Yeah, Sara. You did. You were asking questions, poking, like you wanted to start an argument. Why? Would it be easier on you when I leave if you're pissed at me?"

My eyes fill with tears. That hadn't been my plan at all. I'd just wanted to figure out our future. If we have a future. We've been side-stepping the subject for so long— probably for this exact reason—and I just need an answer...a direction. I can't handle all this uncertainty. I'm a planner. Planners don't fly by the seat of their pants. I need to know if the man I've been falling for sees himself with me beyond these next few days.

"I'm sorry...I didn't mean..."

He steps up to me and takes my face in his hands. "No, I'm sorry. Please don't cry. I know we need to figure this out, but I don't know what to say. I don't know what the right thing to do here is. Neither of us wants to leave home, so where does that leave us?"

"But can't you do your job from anywhere? Why do you have to be in Charlotte?"

He lets go of my face and takes a step back. "My family is there. The band is there."

"I know that. But it just seems like if one of us is going to have to travel, you'd be the more logical choice. I mean why should I uproot my life and go to Charlotte when you'll just end up leaving there for a few months when you go on tour?"

"It's still my home base."

"Why can't this be your home base?"

"Alex and Ally are in Charlotte."

"They're grownups, Trevor."

"You think I don't know that?" he asks defensively. "Look, we're all each other has. They need me."

"Maybe not as much as you think they do," I say quietly.

"What the hell is that supposed to mean?"

I shrink back from his raised voice and look down the beach to make sure Georgie and Gwen are unaffected. They're still digging in the sand for treasures. I look back to Trevor and shrug my shoulders. "I'm just saying, maybe you need them more than they need you."

"What?"

"You've been playing the caregiver role for so long, Trevor, that maybe you haven't realized they don't need you to be their caregiver anymore."

"Bullshit," he spits out, his face twisted into a grimace.

"It's a crutch. You use them as a crutch."

"Shut up. You don't know anything."

I wince, but keep pushing. "If you're not taking care of your family, you don't know what to do."

"That's rich coming from you."

"And I realize that! Who do you think made me realize that? This month with you, I've done more for *me* than I have in a long time. God, Trevor, I just want you to realize the same thing. Do something for you."

He laughs, but it's not a nice laugh. It's dry and full of derision. "And that something I do for *me* is staying here with *you*." The emphasis he puts on "you" is filled with disgust.

How quickly this went south. I shake my head, looking down at the sand beneath my toes. I knew it was bound to happen. I'd warned myself before I even started speaking. I just never guessed that Trevor would get so upset about it. He's always been so reasonable, I had no reason to think he wouldn't be reasonable now.

"Yeah, so I think I'd better go," he says suddenly.

I look up at him, but he quickly looks away and starts walking towards the kids. I watch as he kisses Gwen on the forehead and ruffles Georgie's hair. They both wave at him as he walks away. He pauses in front of me, still not making eye contact. My heart is breaking. Is this it? Is this goodbye?

"I need some time," he says. As I close my eyes and nod, a tear drips down my cheek. "Don't cry, pretty girl." He gently kisses my forehead.

When I open my eyes, he's gone.

Chapter Thirty-Seven

Sara

It's been radio silence from Trevor ever since he left me on the beach. I cried myself to sleep that night and spent all day yesterday wallowing in self-pity. I know I got defensive and crossed the line talking about him and his siblings, but he wasn't exactly innocent either. It took me hours to make that determination and stop beating myself up over the whole thing. We both obviously feel pretty passionate—or stubborn—about our homes, even though relocating would be somewhere in the very distant future. It's just hard not to think about the future when planning the present, at least for me. That's all I'd been trying to do.

Tomorrow is my birthday. We'd planned to spend the day together at his house—a combination birthday-slash-going-away party since they're leaving early Monday morning to drive home. Our argument created a big, black cloud over what should have been a fun, albeit bittersweet, occasion.

I touch up my lip gloss and look at myself in the mirror.

You can do this. Just apologize.

When I woke up this morning, I decided to revert back to Plan A. One month and then goodbye. It's apparent Trevor and I aren't going to agree on a future beyond his visit to the Outer Banks. I never should have brought those things up the other day, I just thought there was enough between us now that we could come to some amicable agreement. Now, I've decided to throw caution to the wind and embrace these last few hours with him. It's not like I'll be bumping into him around town or anything. I should be able to get over him pretty fast.

Right.

So I'm getting ready to head to his house and offer the proverbial olive branch. To apologize—even though I don't necessarily think I was wrong—and take advantage of the little time I have left with him. If he'll have me.

***

I park in the empty driveway and cut off the engine. I hope they haven't already left. My chest tightens and my eyes fill at the thought that I literally might not ever see him again. In the flesh, at least. I'm sure I'll be seeing him on television and online for the rest of my life. My oh-so-lonely life.

Stepping out of the Jeep, I blink my eyes to drive the tears away and take a deep breath. *Maybe they're just out*, I think as the gravel crunches under my feet. They only have one vehicle and there's quite a few of them, so it's possible *someone* is home. Unsure of how much Trevor shared with his family about us—they *are* close—I'm a little nervous about coming head-to-head with anyone *but* Trevor. Hell, I'm nervous about seeing him, too.

Here goes nothing.

I quickly climb the stairs to the front door and knock before I have the chance to psych myself out.

Ten seconds...

I ring the bell.

Twenty seconds...

Thirty seconds...

I knock again.

Forty seconds...

I back away from the door, twisting my hands in front of me. I bite my lip as my eyes fill, yet again. Seems like all I've done in the past twenty-four hours is cry.

He's not here. He's gone. Maybe for good.

I turn away from the door and sit down on the top step, resting my forehead on my knees and letting the tears flow.

I didn't get to say goodbye.

I quietly sob for a minute before I sit up. I wipe the tears from my cheeks and straighten out my hair. I can't believe he just left. We have one little argument and he cuts his vacation short? It wasn't even *that* big of a deal. I can't believe he'd have his family pack up and leave just because he's being a stubborn ass.

I growl as I get to my feet and angrily stomp down the steps, kicking at a rock when I reach the driveway.

"Ow! Shit!" I didn't think that one through, seeing as I'm wearing sandals.

"Are you finished?"

Shrieking in surprise, I turn to face the house...to face the person intruding on my private little hissy fit. I must not have heard him open the door when I was stomping down the steps like a child. His hair is wet, so I guess he'd been in the shower when I knocked.

We stand there staring at each other—me at the bottom of the steps with my red eyes, blotchy cheeks, and swollen toe, and him just outside the front door looking all clean, sexy, and indifferent—for minutes, hours, days...I don't know.

He's still here.

"I thought I heard the bell when I was in the shower."

Yep. He was in the shower. Now I'm picturing him naked. And wet. I clench my thighs together. The big jerk notices and smirks. I growl again.

"Did you need something?" he asks, now descending the stairs very, very slowly.

"I could use some ice for my toe," I say, mentally facepalming myself.

He raises one perfectly manicured eyebrow—it's unfair really—and keeps moving toward me. "Is that all?"

I shake my head.

"What else?" he asks as he stops just inches from me. I can smell his soap and feel his body heat. Every breath he releases sends a tiny minty breeze across my face.

"You...I need you."

He takes a deep, relieving breath and crushes his body into mine. "I need you, too," he says, just before he kisses me.

"I'm so sorry," I mumble against his mouth.

"Me, too," he says as he peppers tiny kisses along my jawline and down my neck. He kisses the tears off my cheeks. He puts his hands on my hips and starts leading me back towards the house. "Everyone is out grabbing lunch," he says as he tightens his grip and lifts me up. I immediately wrap my legs around his waist and he turns and climbs the steps with me wrapped around him. I tighten my grip, afraid we'll fall and he coos, "It's okay, I have you."

And he does have me.

Twice.

Chapter Thirty-Eight

Trevor

To say I've been moody since arguing with Sara the other night would be an understatement. My family pretty much steered clear of me for thirty-six hours straight. I didn't tell them what was up, but I'm sure they'd guessed it had something to do with Sara. I shouldn't have reacted the way I did on the beach, but she hit a nerve. To suggest that my family didn't need me? That I was the one who needed them? It was bullshit. She doesn't know me. She doesn't know them. She doesn't know our history. Who is she to make those accusations?

Nevertheless, her words had me second guessing everything. I spent the last day or so analyzing the dynamic between me and my siblings. Was she right? Then I'd remember all the times Ally, Alex, Joey, and even Evie, have come to me for help or advice, and it erased every seed of doubt her words had planted.

When she showed up at the house yesterday, I was grateful. Grateful, and maybe a little selfish, that at least we'd have a little more time before we had to say goodbye.

"Let's just forget the other night and finish the month together."

As we laid in bed together, her words both relieved me and caused an ache deep in my gut. I thought we'd made progress this month, but it's apparent that we'd taken several steps backwards on the beach. It sucks. It hurts and it sucks, but it's just as well, I suppose. We're both too loyal to our own commitments to come to a compromise, and rather than have that spoil our remaining time together, I'm going to enjoy it while it lasts.

Today is Sara's twenty-sixth birthday. She's spending the day with the twins before dropping them off with Victoria for the night—she hadn't wanted to confuse or upset them with goodbyes—then we're having her over for dinner to celebrate her birthday and our last night of vacation. We leave early in the morning to return to Charlotte. Part of me is happy to return home, but another part of me isn't ready to leave her yet. We already tried to go down that road, though, and it resulted in near disaster. I'm just going to soak up every moment of this last day.

Alex and I are cutting up fruits and veggies, Chase is marinating the steaks, Ally is working on a dry rub for the ribs—Joey applies said rub—and Evie is making a salad. Max is chilling out in front of the TV.

"So...this is it, huh?" Alex says as he decimates a celery stalk. I don't have to ask to know what he's talking about. It's what's on everyone's mind, but no one wants to be the first to mention it. Leave it to Alex.

I shrug. "We knew at the beginning this was all that it was. A summer fling."

"We know you really like her," Ally says, listening in on our quiet conversation from across the large kitchen. It's like she has bat sonar or something.

"What's not to like?" She's sweet, funny, adventurous, easygoing, gorgeous...

Evie agrees with Ally. "We really like her, too."

"Well, it is what it is. Just a summer fling. That's it."

"Maybe you can keep in touch," Chase offers.

Yeah...maybe...

***

"Y'all, this it too much!" Sara says, holding her hands over her cheeks to hide her blush. Chase just carried out the huge cake Ally had slaved over early this morning.

"It's not just your birthday cake," Ally tells her, bumping her with her hip. "It's a celebration cake. We're celebrating your birthday, friendship, family, and all the fun we've had this month."

"It says 'Happy Birthday Sara' on it," Sara deadpans.

Ally laughs. "Well, I couldn't exactly fit everything I wanted to say on it."

"Thank you," Sara says as she embraces Ally.

The ache in my chest gets stronger. Sara fits. She fits so well into my life. She gets along with my family. It's like she's one of us. I know I've said it before, but this sucks. Why can't we just get our heads out of our asses and work this shit out? Maybe we can give it time and, like Chase said, keep in touch. Maybe absence will make the heart grow fonder or some shit.

Maybe...

***

I pull the van into Sara's driveway later that night. We had a great time with my family, but now I think we're both ready for some alone time. I had picked Sara up from her house earlier, so that I would have an

- 278 -

excuse to go back to her house with her. I wasn't kidding anyone at the house; they all knew what I was up to. The only downfall is I can't be out all night since we have to pack up the van early in the morning.

I make her wait and run around to her side of the car to open her door. "My lady," I say and she laughs at my cheesiness.

I'm gonna miss her laugh.

We make our way into her house, hand-in-hand. I'm afraid to hold on too tight—I might hurt her, but I don't want to let go either.

I'm gonna miss the way she feels.

"Want something to drink?" she asks. "Wine? Beer? Water?"

"I could really go for a beer," I tell her. Maybe it'll settle my nerves. I feel like a teenage boy on his first date. This is Sara. Why am I nervous?

She smiles at me before heading to the fridge, grabbing two beers, and popping the tops.

I'm gonna miss her smile.

Leaning back against the kitchen counter, side-by-side, we drink our beers in silence. It's like all the words in the world have already been spoken. There's nothing left to say but goodbye, and neither of us wants to say that. Not yet. Maybe not ever.

I chug the rest of my beer and set it on the counter, then turn to her. She's looking up at me with sad, doe eyes, and it nearly breaks my heart. I pull her into my chest and kiss the top of her head. She smells like her...coconut and vanilla.

I'm gonna miss her smell.

"I'm gonna miss you so much," she sniffles.

"Ditto, pretty girl. Ditto."

Chapter Thirty-Nine

Sara

I pull away from Trevor's chest and look up into his dark blue eyes. "Make love to me," I whisper.

He shuts his eyes so tight I can see the creases at the sides. When he opens them again, what I see there must be what he sees in mine. Pain. Sadness. Complete and utter misery. This is going to break both of us.

He leans in and kisses me, his lips soft but firm. It soon turns demanding, and he lifts me up. I wrap my legs around his waist as he carries me through the house and up the stairs to my bedroom. He sets me down at the foot of the bed, and we both make quick work of our clothes. He stands just a foot away from me and his heated gaze takes me in from head to toe and back again. Like he's memorizing me.

Maybe he is.

Less than a moment goes by before he's on me. His hands are in my hair, mine are on his ass, pulling his erection against my core. We fall to the bed in a tangled heap, unable to break the kiss that fuses us together. We're desperate...hungry. He reaches for a condom I hadn't even seen him toss on the bed and quickly rolls it on. This isn't the love making I had anticipated—hoped for—this is pure, carnal desire.

I cry out as he thrusts into me, and he swallows my moans with his kisses. He spreads my legs further apart and pushes them up to my chest. The new position has him deeper and deeper with each pound of his hips. I feel myself clamping down on him, the sensations overwhelming, and he begins to grind himself against me. It's too much...the build...the rise...and the fall. Moments later, we both come, crying out each other's name.

He collapses on top of me, sweaty and breathless. "I'm sorry."

Sorry? "Why the hell are you sorry? That was amazing," I pant out.

He chuckles and kisses my forehead before rolling off of me. He takes care of the condom and pulls me against his side. "I meant to make love to you, but once I had my hands on you…"

"Never apologize for *that*. It was perfect." *You're perfect.*

He smiles. "I guess that just means we'll have to do it again," he says.

"I love the way you think," I tell him, nuzzling my nose against his chest.

He turns his head and kisses me, this time softer and with less urgency. I climb on top of him and continue the kiss, running my hands up and down his body. He rolls us over and looks into my eyes like he's about to say something, then just gives me a small smile and kisses me again. He kisses and touches me all over. Making love to my body with his hands and mouth before finally taking me again. This time it's slow and it's sweet and when it's over, I can't hold in the tears that fall.

***

The moon is bright in the cloudless sky, lighting up the beach as if it were daylight. We walk across the smooth sand, hand-in-hand, neither one of us wanting to let the other go. Not yet. We stop at the shoreline, and Trevor stands behind me, wrapping his arms around my waist and resting his chin on my shoulder. I lean my head against his.

This is it.

This is the end.

It's close to midnight, and they're heading out early in the morning. He had assured me that he wasn't driving home and therefore could stay out as late as he wanted, but I'm not sure how long we should prolong the inevitable.

"Alex, Ally, and I came here once with our parents when we were kids. It's why we chose this place this summer."

"That's nice," I tell him. And it is nice that he was able to make new memories here with his siblings.

"I wish they were here," he says somberly. "My mom would love you."

I squeeze his hands, which are knotted in front of my belly. "I would have loved to meet her."

"This sucks," he says as he lets me go and takes a step back. I close my eyes, willing myself to have enough strength to say goodbye to him and not stowaway in the back of his van and abandon all of my responsibilities.

Keep your cool, Sara. Be strong...you've been training for shit like this your whole life.

I hear Trevor's footsteps, and I turn to look, seeing him pick up a large stick a few yards away. He comes back to me and touches the stick to the sand. He fiddles with it for a minute, then steps back so I can see what he's done. He drew a big heart in the sand. A lone tear escapes my eye and drips down my cheek. He hands me the stick.

"Now draw yours."

More tears break free as I draw my own heart, overlapping his. He takes the stick from me and tosses it back in the direction he got it from. Then he pulls me into his chest.

"I'm going to miss you, pretty girl."

"I'm going to miss you, too," I say back, proud of myself for being able to get the words out without sobbing.

"You have my number," he starts but stops when he feels me shaking my head.

"No, Trevor," I tell him. "This has to end here...tonight."

He pulls away from me and looks at me like he can't believe what he heard. But he heard right. The truth is...I'll never get over him if we stay in touch. Never. And if we try again, we'll still be left with the same obstacles we argued about before. Nothing has changed in that regard.

"But...Sara..."

"Let's just remember this," I say, leaning back into him and wrapping my arms around him. "Let's remember all the fun times we've had this month. The first time we saw each other...the first time we heard each other laugh...our first touch...first kiss...first everything else... Let's just hold on to those memories."

"Fuck," he swears quietly as he tightens his hold on me. "I'll never forget you. Never." He tips his head down and kisses me, hard and quick. Then he lets go and walks away.

I watch him walk away with tears streaming down my face, and when he's finally out of view, I fall to my knees, sobbing beside our hearts in the sand.

Chapter Forty

Trevor

I kiss her and hold her close, telling her I'll never forget her. Then I walk away, one last time, leaving my heart intertwined with hers in the sand.

The next day we leave the Outer Banks, and I feel like I've left a piece of myself—of my soul—behind.

Chapter Forty-One

Sara

Two months later

"Well?" Victoria says, tapping her fingernail on my desk.

I shake my head; the spreadsheets in front of me are a complete blur. "I'm sorry," I sigh.

"You weren't paying attention, were you?" she accuses, narrowing her eyes at me from her seat on the other side of my desk.

I slowly shake my head. "I'm sorry, Vic."

For the first time in years I have no responsibilities, other than my business, for an entire weekend. I should be focused. But I'm not. I can't stop wondering how the twins are doing on their first weekend visit with their mother in years. They cried when she picked them up in a newer model sedan I'd never seen before. The image of their tearful faces in the back window as the taillights faded down the driveway will not leave my mind. Neither will the dreadful feeling that I may never see them again.

It's a silly notion, though. My sister isn't *that* stupid. She knows she's on thin ice with the courts, and violating the visitation agreement would be a major step in the wrong direction. Still, I can't believe the judge even honored the agreement in the first place, given her record. But she did well in the supervised visitations so this was the next logical step. Whatever.

Everyone deserves a second chance.

I hear my mother's wise words in my head. She's right. If she hadn't believed that, she never would have adopted my sister and me twenty plus years ago. It's just so difficult giving Nora the benefit of the doubt when she's done nothing in the past six years to earn it. Especially where the twins are concerned.

"It's Jerry. I think we're going to need to fire him. Called out twice last week and the one day he actually showed up, he got one tour stuck and the other came back an hour late. The guests on both tours were not happy."

I frown. I built this business from the ground up; it physically pains me to hear guests didn't enjoy their experience.

"And I think Jeanette deserves a raise. Or a promotion or something. She handled the disgruntled guests beautifully. She's always going above and beyond her regular receptionist duties. Of course, if we didn't have morons like Jerry on staff, she wouldn't have to."

I snort, which Vic clearly doesn't appreciate. "I wholeheartedly agree with you. You're the Assistant Manager; I obviously trust your judgement, Vic. If you say he needs to go, then he needs to go. And if you say Jeanette should get a raise, I believe you. I trust you. I wish we could promote her, but there just isn't a slot she can easily transition into, but maybe that's something we can work on developing. In the meantime, a raise will do. Who knows? She may not even want more responsibility."

Victoria nods in agreement, then cocks her head to the side. "You okay?"

I sigh. "I just thought I'd hear from the kids by now," I say, looking at the clock. It's now seven at night, and Nora picked them up at eight this morning.

"Why don't you call them?"

"I'm trying to give her the benefit of the doubt. If I call, she's going to think I'm checking in and that I don't trust her."

"But you don't trust her," she points out.

"I know. But I'm trying." And I really, really am. "I want the twins to have a positive relationship with their mother. If there is unease between Nora and me, it'll rub off on them and I don't want them to feel anxious when they have to spend time with her." I also don't want her to have any reason to keep them from me if she does end up with permanent custody.

"You're a bigger person than me," Vic mumbles.

My cell phone rings, and I reach across my desk to grab it.

"See, that's probably them there."

I look at the screen and immediately see it's not Nora's number. The area code is 704. I only know one person with that area code, one group of people actually, and I wasn't sure I'd ever hear from them again after the way we left things.

"Aren't you going to answer it?"

I glare at Vic but curiosity gets the best of me, and I swipe the screen to accept the call. "Hello?"

"Auntie?" a small voice says.

"Georgie?" My eyes widen, and my spine stiffens. What the hell is he doing calling me from a Charlotte number? I swear if my sister left them with someone…

"Auntie, we're scared," he cries, and my heart breaks.

"Georgie, sweetheart, what's going on? Where is Gwen? Where's your mom?" My pulse is racing, and I feel every muscle in my body tense as I await his response.

"Gwen is here with me. Nora left."

"What do you mean she left?" I yell, immediately cursing myself for doing so when Georgie's cries become louder. Not the way to soothe an upset child. "I'm sorry, Georgie. I didn't mean to yell. Where are you, baby? Do you know?"

"I don't know," he sobs. "We drove for a really long while. We're at a hotel. Like the one we stayed at when we went to visit Grammy and Pop that time."

"Ok, sweetheart. Do the doors open to the parking lot or a hallway?"

"Parking lot."

I clench my fists and close my eyes; it takes everything in me not to scream. I was so *stupid* letting them leave with her! Opening my eyes, I see Victoria sitting across from me, wide-eyed, mouthing something. "What?" I whisper.

"The phone number. Google the phone number. If he's calling from a landline, it should come up."

Right!

"Listen, Georgie. I'm going to come get you. I just need to figure out where you are, okay? I'm not going to hang up. I'm going to stay on the phone with you the whole time, okay?"

"Yes." His voice sounds so small, even younger than his six years. "It's getting dark, Auntie," he whimpers.

My *fucking* sister. I'm going to kill her when I find her.

"I'm going to be there with you before that happens, okay? I promise." I pull the phone away from my face and quickly jot down the ten digits.

"Please hurry. There are lots of noises outside."

The tears of fear and frustration finally leak from my eyes, making my computer screen blur as I type the numbers into the search engine. The name "Rest Motor Lodge" pops up, as well as the address and the city. Charlotte.

They're six hours away.

"What the hell is she doing with them in Charlotte?" Victoria whispers, echoing my own thoughts.

Only I know the answer to that question. My worst fear confirmed. She was running with them. It's no surprise she couldn't make it farther than six hours before needing to stop for a fix of something. She probably had no clue the twins knew how to use a phone, let alone had my cell number memorized. Smartest thing I ever did.

"Georgie?"

"Yes," he sniffles.

"I know where you are. Okay, baby?"

"Yes. You'll be here soon?" he asks, his voice sounding so hopeful.

"I'm going to get there as fast as I can. And I'm going to stay on the phone with you the entire time, okay?"

"Yes."

"Why don't you tell me the things you saw out the window while you were in the car?"

As he started talking about the various wildlife and different colors and models of cars he saw on the trip, I put the phone on speaker, then mute, and began searching my contacts.

"What are you doing?" Victoria asks.

"I can't leave them alone in that motel for six hours while they wait for me to get there."

"So who are you calling?"

"The only person I know besides the two of us who will drop everything and be there."

Chapter Forty-Two

Trevor

As I pull into the parking lot of Lombardi's, Ally's favorite restaurant, my cell phone rings. I disconnect it from the vehicle's blue tooth so I can get out of the car.

"Hello?" I answer, not recognizing the number.

"Trevor?"

"Sara?" *What the hell?*

"Thank God, Trevor." I can hear the tears in her voice. Whatever has her calling me when she said I'd never hear from her again obviously has her in a panic.

"Are you okay? What's wrong?"

"I need your help. Are you home?"

"I'm meeting Chase and Ally for dinner," I say, looking around the packed parking lot for their cars.

"Are you in Charlotte, Trevor?" she cries.

"Yes. What's this about?"

"The twins. Nora took off with them."

"What?" My blood runs cold at her words. No wonder she's freaking out. *I'm* freaking out.

"They're in Charlotte. Georgie called me from a motel because my sister left them alone there. They've been alone for hours, and it's dark and Gwen hates the dark. They're really scared."

"Do you know the name of the motel?"

"Rest Motor Lodge," she says.

"I know where that is," I say, withholding the fact that it's in the dingiest, most disgusting part of town. The only reason I know where the place is because it borders the industrial neighborhood where our recording studio is. "What's the room number?"

"Hold on." I hear mumbled conversation between her and maybe Georgie? "Georgie thinks it's room 124. I've got him on the line on my cell phone."

"I'm on my way. I'll be there in less than ten minutes."

She sniffles on the line and it breaks my heart. "Thank you, Trevor. Thank you so much."

"It's alright, I got this. Talk to Georgie. Stay on the line with him. Tell him to count the knocks when he hears them. I'll knock ten times. Okay?"

"Yes," she whispers.

"I'll be there soon." I hang up without saying good-bye. I'm not sure I can ever say goodbye to Sara again; the first time was hard enough.

I get back into my car and start it up, before I can get it in gear, there's a knock on my window. I look up and see Ally's smiling face.

"A little impatient there, brother?" she smiles as I roll down the window. Her smile turns to a frown when she sees the tortured expression on my face. "Trevor, what is it? What's wrong? Is it Alex?"

I shake my head. "No. I just got a call from Sara. Her sister took off with the kids. They're here in Charlotte. She needs me to go get them." Ally runs around the front of the car and opens the passenger door. "What are you doing?"

"I'm going with you. Who knows what condition those kids are in, you need all the help you can get. Gwen and I bonded this summer. She'll be happy to see me." Ally buckles her seat belt and pats the dashboard. "Let's go!"

I look at my little sister in awe as she taps around the screen of her cell phone, then raises it to her ear.

"What?" she asks, looking at me with one eyebrow raised.

I shake my head and smile at her as I pull out of the parking space and turn out of the parking lot. "Nothing, kid. I'm just one of the luckiest guys in the world to have you as my sister."

She rolls her eyes. "Hey, baby," she coos into the phone. She must have called Chase. "I'm not at the restaurant. Change of plans. I'm with Trevor. We're both fine, but Trevor got a call from Sara, and the twins are here in Charlotte. Her sister took them. We're going to get them." She's quiet for a moment before asking me the name of the hotel. I tell her, and she cringes. When she tells Chase the name, I hear him curse through the phone. I hope I can get those kids out of that place without Sara having to see it.

Ally hangs up the phone. "Chase is meeting us there. He was just leaving the studio anyway so he'll probably beat us there." Chase had been working on laying down some of the guitar tracks for the new album this afternoon.

There's a comfortable silence between Ally and me for a few minutes. Each lost in our own thoughts as the scenery passes by in a blur.

Ally is the first to speak. "What do you think this means?"

"What does what mean?"

"Her calling you out of the blue like that. I mean it's been what? Two months without contact?"

My sister, ever the optimist, always trying to find the silver lining. "It means nothing, Ally. She's in a bind, and she needs help. If were any other city in the world, she wouldn't have called me."

"She could have called the police," Ally offers.

"And scare Georgie and Gwen more than they already are?"

Ally shrugs. "If she really never wanted to see or speak to you again, she would have found another option. She wouldn't have called you. I think she still cares for you."

"To *still* care about me, she would have had to care about me before," I say through a clenched jaw, tightening my hands on the steering wheel.

"You don't think she did?" Ally looks at me in shock.

"Maybe she did, but it obviously wasn't enough." Ally winces back in her seat. *Shit.* Now I've stuck my foot in it. "It's not the same as you and Chase," I tell her.

"Isn't it worse, though?" she asks softly. "I fell in love with him, forgot him, fell in love with him again, and then pushed him away. For years, Trevor. Not just days or weeks or months, but years. And Chase waited. All that time...he waited."

"Because he loved you."

"He did...he does. Even when I didn't deserve it."

"Hey," I start, but she cuts me off.

"Trevor, I don't care what you say, or what Chase says, or anyone else for that matter. I didn't deserve his patience. I love him, and I am forever grateful that he loved me enough to wait while I sorted my shit out because we're together now, and I'm really, truly happy. But he didn't have to. And that's neither here nor there. My point is, I know what it's like to care about someone and to be so scared you end up making a snap decision. Then throw pride and independence into the mix and...it can get messy, Trev."

Pride and independence. If those words didn't perfectly describe Sara, nothing did.

"I get it, okay?" I tell her. "But I still don't think I ever would have heard from her again had the twins not ended up here."

Ally shrugs. "Maybe it's a sign."

I glare at her. "That's a really twisted sign, Al."

Speaking of twisted...I turn on my blinker and pull into the parking lot of Rest Motor Lodge. The structure looks like it belongs in a catalog of abandoned buildings. There is only one functioning street lamp in the parking lot, and it's flickering.

"Look for 124," I tell Ally. Headlights flashing to my left startle me, but it's just Chase. He pulls out of his spot and follows me down to the other end of the lot where I park in front of a dingy green door with a sideways metal plate that reads "124," the "4" hanging at an odd angle.

Ally shudders. "I can't believe those kids are in there. They must be terrified."

We get out of the car and meet Chase at the door. I hold my index finger up to my lips, indicating quiet, then knock on the door. On the tenth knock the door flies open and two little bodies slam into my legs. Careful not to knock them down, I squat down to their level and wrap my arms around them. They're shuddering against me, clearly scared out of their minds.

I look up at Ally and tilt my head in the direction of the phone laying on the bed...Sara's probably on the other end of that phone, losing her mind. I watch Ally take the phone and speak. Her eyes well up with tears as she nods and continues to speak to her. She makes eye contact with me, and mouths "She wants to talk to you." I nod.

"Hey," I say, pulling back a little. Georgie looks up at me, but Gwen stays burrowed in my side. "Did you see who came with me to see you?" I ask with a smile. When Georgie looks behind me and sees Chase, a small smile tugs at the corner of his mouth.

"And remember Ally? She's right behind you." That causes Gwen to perk up. She lifts her tearstained face and turns her head. Ally gives them a little wave, and I am completely forgotten. Both kids fly over to my sister, and she wraps her arms around them, giving me a "told you so" wink.

I stand up and walk over to the phone. "They're okay," I tell Sara.

Her quiet sobs nearly undo me. "Thank you. I don't know what I would have done if you weren't there."

"You probably would have broken every traffic law from the coast to here trying to make it."

"You're probably right," she laughed softly.

"Look, the kids are okay. They're safe. I'm not going to let them out of my sight. Why don't you concentrate on driving for now, okay? You can call whenever you want, as often as you'd like, but just give me a few minutes so we can call the police and get the kids out of here."

"The police? You said they were okay!" she shouts in my ear.

"Calm down, Sara. They are okay. But what happens if your sister comes back here and calls the cops because the kids are missing?"

"Serves her right! I can't believe she did this. I can't believe she tried to take off with them and then has the nerve to leave them by themselves!"

Well, an angry Sara is definitely better than a crying Sara. Though she's not any easier to try to calm down.

"Sara. Sara!"

"Sorry," she says quietly.

"We'll call the cops and explain the situation. That way if she tries to file a report, they'll know what their dealing with and won't be sent on a wild goose chase."

"I just can't believe this is happening," she sighs.

"I know, babe, we'll figure it out." I look across the room to where the twins are in quiet conversation with Chase and Ally, smiles on all their faces. "The important thing is that the kids are okay. They're talking to Ally and Chase right now, and they look real happy."

"Thank you."

"You're welcome. Now let me call the cops. They'll probably need to talk to you when they get here, too."

Chapter Forty-Three

Sara

It's the middle of the night when I finally turn down the dark streets of Pleasant Pointe. The scattered streetlamps are absolutely no help in reading the street names and house numbers. Finally, I locate the two-story brick home nestled in a cul-de-sac and pull into the wraparound driveway. I park behind a shiny black Range Rover, next to a brand new red Corvette. Must be nice, the rock star life...

I hop out of the car and quickly make my way up the brick path to the front door. I briefly take in the outside of the home. It's very simple and modest, red brick with black shutters framing the windows. It's not at all what I'd expect a few twenty-something rock stars to live in. I vaguely recall Evie, or was it Ally, saying something about Trevor and Alex living in their parents' house. That would explain it.

The path curves around some shrubs, and I pause when I see a figure hunched on the steps. The person rises and takes a step towards me, and in the yellow glow of the porch light, I see it's Alex.

"You scared the hell out of me, Alex." I say with a hand over my chest.

"Think I was a ghost?" he smirks.

"I don't know what I thought," I mumble. My body feels like lead. It's like the anxiety and exhaustion that has been building up over the last several hours has finally unleashed itself on my body.

Alex, rather perceptive, notices. "You okay?" He steps forward and puts his arm around my shoulder.

"Just tired. The twins still asleep?" I ask, moving forward again with his assistance.

He nods. "They've been passed out in Ally's old room since about thirty minutes after we got them here. After they devoured an entire pizza in front of the TV, of course."

I frown and fresh tears fill my eyes. Those poor kids. Tired, hungry, scared, and alone. I can't even imagine how they must have been feeling. When I get my hands on my sister...

Alex quietly opens the front door, and we make our way inside. "It's an old house," he whispers. "Lots of creaks and echoes."

I nod and carefully follow him across the foyer to the stairs. As I climb the steps behind Alex, I wonder where Trevor is.

Maybe he doesn't want to see you, the nagging little voice in my head says. If that's the case, I deserve it. He'd wanted something...anything...and I couldn't give it to him. Wouldn't give it to him.

"They're in here," Alex whispers once we reach the second floor. He's standing at the second door on the right. "If you're hungry, I can fix you a snack."

I smile at him. "Thanks, but I think I'm just gonna crash with them."

I catch Alex give me a funny look before he nods and heads back down the stairs. Not sure what that was about, I just shake it off and turn the knob, then slowly push open the door. Keeping my eyes on the ground, I slip inside and quietly close the door behind me. When I finally look up at the bed, my breath catches.

In the moonlight, I see that Trevor is fast asleep, lying on his back in the middle of the full-size bed, with Georgie and Gwen clinging to his sides. I lean back against the closed door and slide to the ground.

They're safe.

Tears of frustration, terror, exhaustion, and joy drip down my face, and I fight back the sobs. I really don't want to wake them up. Any of them.

They're safe.

They're sleeping.

They're okay.

I lean my head against my knees and wrap my arms around my legs, letting the silent sobs take me.

I'm not sure how long I sit like that before I feel his hands on my shoulders. I pick my head up, and through watery vision I can just make out Trevor's concerned face. His eyebrows are scrunched up in that way they are when he's upset or confused. Just one of the things I learned about him in our short time together.

Another sob, this one louder, breaks through the invisible barrier, and he pulls me into his chest, shushing me.

"It's okay," he repeats over and over again. "They're okay."

I fist his shirt in my hands and let it all out. All my fears about the kids and insecurities about myself pour out. The sadness and loneliness I've felt since Trevor and I said what was supposed to have been our final goodbye.

He pulls me in closer and rubs his hands up my back, soothing me. I miss his touch...his smell...his voice...his everything.

I miss...*him.*

Once I calm down he pulls away, running his hand down the side of my face before letting me go. I feel incomplete. But what can I say or do? I made my bed. Now I have to lie in it.

"Thank you," I whisper.

He silently nods, and we both rise from the floor. He looks over to the twins, still sleeping soundly, then gestures towards the door. I nod and quietly follow him out.

"I don't know how to thank you," I tell him. "If they had ended up anywhere else, I don't know what I would have done. Thank you for going to them...for taking them here."

He shakes his head. "No need to thank me. I'd do anything for them."

My heart melts, and it burns at the same time. At one point he'd said he would do anything for me, too. I guess I gave up that right when I gave him up.

Why did I do that again? Oh yeah! Because I'm a stubborn ass who can do everything on her own and wouldn't know a compromise if it slapped me in the face...that's why.

"I hate to ask, but do you mind if I rest for a little bit? I just need a little nap and then we'll hit the road first thing in the morning."

Trevor looks at me like I'm crazy. Maybe I am. "Sara, it's four o'clock in the morning. You don't need rest, you need sleep. You've been driving all night and you're exhausted."

My eyes widen, I hadn't even realized it was that late. I must have fallen asleep on the floor in the bedroom.

"I didn't realize..." I trail off, a little too exhausted to make verbal sense.

He opens a door behind him, across the hall from the twins. "You can sleep in here. That way they won't wake you when they get up...or while they're sleeping. They both kick."

I smile a little at that. They are the worst bed buddies.

"It's okay. I'd rather be with them." And never let them out of my sight again.

He nods, understanding the direction of my thoughts. "Of course."

I turn and put my hand on the doorknob, then look over my shoulder at him. The heat from his gaze startles me. But as quickly as I notice it, it's gone.

"Thank you...for everything."

"You're welcome, Sara." He watches me step into the bedroom, and we make eye contact once more before I close the door. The heat is still there in his eyes...barely.

I wonder what that means...

Chapter Forty-Four

Sara

The bright light pouring through the sheer lavender curtains causes me to stir. For a moment, I forget where I am. Taking in the purple room, I recall the events of last night...the events that brought me to Trevor's house.

Trevor. God, he looked so good last night. Even better than I'd remembered.

I sit up straight when I realize I'm alone in the bed.

The twins!

I fly off the bed and run to the bedroom door. As I open the door, the smells of bacon and something sweet waft through the air. I start to run down the stairs and slow down when I hear that familiar laughter.

They're safe. They're okay.

I repeat the mantra that kept me sane when I'd arrived last night. I proceed down the steps and my nose leads me through the house and to the kitchen. Standing in the doorway, I observe the scene in front of me. Georgie and Gwen are sitting on stools at the island in the center of the kitchen, their chins resting in their little hands and elbows leaning on the black granite countertops. Ally is at the stove flipping pancakes. Beside her is Trevor, frying up bacon and eggs.

In the darkness and chaos of the previous evening, I hadn't even considered the potential awkwardness this visit would bring in the bright light of day. I'd been so focused on getting here, on the twins' safety that I hadn't even considered what it would be like to see Trevor's family again. I'm not worried about the kids, they are innocent. But me? Not so much. It's quite possible I'd broken their brother's heart.

Ally turns around and catches sight of me in the doorway. I offer a shy smile and look away towards the twins. I'm not expecting her acceptance, so when she runs over and embraces me, I'm caught off guard. I tentatively wrap my arms around her and return her hug.

"It's so good to see you," she says, smiling, as she pulls away.

"Same," I say and mean it.

Our little reunion is cut short by two little tornadoes running at me full speed. "Auntie Sara!" they shout in unison. I drop down to my knees and hug them both. I feel the tears behind my eyes and tightly close them.

Be strong for the kids!

That's my other mantra.

I pull back and look them both over. No visible damage, thank goodness...but the emotional damage...

"Are you two having a good time with Trevor and Ally?" I ask them, careful not to bring their attention back to last night.

"Yes!" Georgie exclaims. "Ally let us help stir the batter for the pancakes."

"And I got to add the chocolate chips!" Gwen adds.

I smile at both of them and look over their shoulders to offer my thanks to Ally and Trevor, but my words get stuck in my throat. Trevor's looking at me again. That look of pure want and need. I quickly look away, engaging myself with the kids again.

"So you had a nice sleepover?" I ask, instantly cursing myself for bring up last night.

Gwen frowns, obviously remembering how they ended up with Trevor last night. But Georgie smiles brightly and rambles on about their ride in Trevor's big fancy car, their pizza dinner, and the latest cartoon flick they got to watch on the huge television in the living room.

"It's on the wall, Auntie!" he tells me.

This excites Gwen, and she grabs my hand and pulls me out of the kitchen so I can see it. Thankful for the reprieve from Trevor's hot stare, I let her. We 'ooh' and 'ahh' over the television and extensive movie collection. The kids tell me how Trevor and Alex told them that Max came over all the time, and that's why they had so many kids' movies.

I'd bet anything Alex watches those movies as much as Max, but I wouldn't dare say it. I think I lost the right to joke around with the family when I pushed Trevor away.

Must it always come back to that?

Yes, because you did push him away.

Sometimes I hate my conscience.

"Breakfast is ready," Ally calls from the kitchen.

The twins take off, and I slowly follow behind, taking in some of the family photographs on the walls. The Monroes are a beautiful family...were a beautiful family, I think as I look at pictures of them with their parents. They all have their mother's hair and coloring, but their dad's features. What a shame to have lost them so young.

I pause at one photograph. It's of a smiling little boy with messy blond hair and dark blue eyes. On each of his sides are newborn infants wrapped in pink and blue. This is the photo Trevor was telling me about, and boy, you can see his elation. I can understand why this is one of his favorite memories. I smile at the little boy in the picture. Trevor was just as handsome back then as he is now, only now he's got that whole sex appeal thing going on. My insides clench.

When I arrive back in the kitchen, I immediately notice that Trevor is absent. Ally sees me looking and offers me a soft smile. I take a seat at the table beside Gwen, and quietly thank Ally for the meal.

"I really appreciate this. You didn't have to make breakfast."

"Well, it's more like lunch," she laughs.

My eyes widen. "Lunch?" I look at the clock on the stove...holy crap, it's after eleven! I haven't slept this late in...four years.

"You were exhausted, so we let you sleep. The kids had a snack this morning and watched some TV with Alex before he left with Chase for the studio. They wanted to wait and have breakfast with you."

I look at my niece and nephew and smile. I raised some good kids.

"Well, thank you. I guess I did need the sleep."

"I can't even imagine what you must have felt last night," she says quietly. The twins are chattering about whatever show they watched this morning, so they pay her no mind.

"It was the single most terrifying experience of my entire life," I admit. Ally nods solemnly, and we continue our meal in silence.

As I'm helping clear the table, I look around once more, wondering where Trevor ran off to. I'd be lying to myself if I said it wasn't my fault he's not here, enjoying breakfast with his sister. I know he's avoiding me...and with good reason.

Ally answers my silent question. "He went for a walk."

I nod. "I'm so very sorry," I tell her as I turn on the sink and start rinsing the syrup off the dishes. For what, I'm not entirely sure. Hurting her brother? Ending our friendship? Being a scared little girl?

"I know," she says, taking a plate from me and placing it in the dishwasher. And I believe that she truly does know. Trevor had told me a little bit of what she and Chase went through before she got her memory back. "But maybe it isn't me you should be saying it to."

I look at her, slightly stunned by her comment.

"He misses you," is all she says.

We continue our routine in silence, but my mind is racing.

He misses me?

He misses me.

He misses me!

I smile and bump Ally's shoulder with mine. When she looks over at me, surprised by the gesture, I smile and tell her, "Thanks."

Chapter Forty-Five

Trevor

I had to get out of there.

Just the sight of Sara made my heart ache. Last night, she'd looked so fragile, so lost. This morning, she'd looked peaceful in her sleep. And when she'd arrived in the kitchen just a little while ago, she'd looked content, and then confused. Like she didn't quite know what to do with herself.

I know it had to be awkward for her to be in my home after the way we left things—after the way she left things. So I did what I thought was best, and took myself out of the equation.

I haven't taken a walk in long time. With how busy my life has become, it's been too easy to forget to slow down and appreciate the simple things. Even while on vacation, we were all still on the go. Playing tourist and trying to enjoy every last bit of freedom before returning to the daily grind of our lives. On top of that, I'd been trying to cram as much time in with Sara as I could.

And for what?

I've asked myself that question almost every day since we left the Outer Banks. I know what she and I had agreed to. We both knew it had an expiration date. But I couldn't help but want more...need more. Sara had an irresistible quality about her. Hell, she still does. That's why this time, I had to walk away.

An hour passes, then two, as I make my way around the streets my sister, brother, and I played on as children. I passed the homes some of our high school classmates and friends grew up in, most of them off to do bigger and better things. How lucky am I that I get to do bigger and better things right here in my home town?

This is the quintessential American Dream neighborhood. Sidewalks lined with white picket fences, dogs in the yard, bikes in the driveway...I'd be lying if I said that I've never pictured living here with Sara. Teaching the twins to ride a bike on the same street my dad taught me. Watching them run through the sprinklers in the summer like Alex, Ally, and I did.

But that could never happen—would never happen. Sara's life is on the coast, where her business is. Can't exactly do horse tours and beach excursions in Charlotte. I can work from anywhere, but she can't.

I can work from anywhere...

I shake the thought from my head. Not possible. My family is here. Without our mom and dad, Alex and Ally need me.

But do they really?

I stop in my tracks.

Do they really need me?

I start walking back towards my house, a little faster now, reflecting on the past year or so. Ally and Chase are living together and engaged. They're solid. Chase takes care of Ally now, I don't. I think about Alex...he comes and goes as he pleases and spends a lot of time with Joey, Evie, and Max. We still hang out, play video games, and do guy stuff together when we're not at the studio or on tour. But he takes care of himself. Feeds himself. Buys his own clothes and other necessities. Sure, he could use a babysitter every once in a while, but he doesn't *need* me.

Was it ever them who needed me? Or was it always me who needed them?

Maybe Sara was right.

She and I had sort of bonded over that obligation we seemed to share. Only hers was out of pure necessity as the twins were just toddlers. Mine was out of what? Ally and Alex were old enough to take care of themselves. Sure, Ally had needed some extra help in the beginning when she didn't have her memories. But what now?

The answer comes to me simply, though I feel like it should have been with the weight of a thousand bricks.

To fill a void. To fill *the* void my parents left behind when they died. The void I've been pretending doesn't exist for the past five years.

Sara knew, but I didn't listen—or I didn't care to hear it.

I'm a fool. An idiot. Over the past couple months, how many times have Ally and Alex told me to go back to her? How many times did they encourage me to call her? They'd said I looked sad and they knew I missed her. Even Chase, Joey and Evie commented on my mood. I didn't listen. I was so blind—I *am* so blind. They'd all known damn well Sara couldn't leave the Outer Banks. They knew that and yet they still encouraged me to be with her, knowing it could mean separating us—breaking up the family.

I'm only a block away from the house, so I pick up my pace. I have to talk to her. We can make this work. I can stay in Charlotte when we're recording and spend the rest of the time out there with her. When we're on tour...well, I don't know what will happen when we're on tour, but that's not something we need to figure out now.

My steps falter, and my shoulders slump as the house comes in view.

Her Jeep isn't in the driveway.

She's gone.

I can't believe she left without saying goodbye. If she didn't want to see me, at the very least she could have let me say goodbye to Georgie and Gwen.

I trudge up the front steps and enter the house. I hear Ally's laughter coming from the kitchen and want to escape to my bedroom, suddenly feeling exhausted. But a) I'm not going to go hide and sulk, and b) I want to know why the hell she let Sara leave.

I walk through the doorway to the kitchen, and my steps falter for the second time in as many minutes.

She's still here.

Sara looks up at me from her seat at the island, her blue eyes sparkling and gives me a small smile. My eyes are locked on hers, and I barely register Ally excusing herself from the room.

"Hi, Trevor." Her voice is like music to my ears.

She's still here.

"Your Jeep," I say, because I can't seem to form a coherent sentence.

She looks down at the countertop with a frown on her face. "It was making a noise on the drive here. Alex took it to get looked at. I'm sorry."

"Sorry for what?" She could mean a thousand different things.

"I'm sorry if you came back because you thought I was gone. I don't mean to overstay my welcome. It's just Alex offered, and the twins were excited to go for a ride in Chase's car."

I take a tentative step towards her. "I'm not upset that you're still here. I'm glad you are."

She looks up at me then, and I can see her eyes are now shining with unshed tears. As much as I hate to see her sad, it's a good thing. It means she's feeling something.

"You're glad?"

"Yes. We need to talk."

Chapter Forty-Six

Sara

Now those are the four most dreaded words in the English language.

We need to talk.

Doing my best to hide my panic and praying that it's not too late, I nod my agreement.

"Why don't we go out back?" he asks, gesturing towards the glass doors that lead out to the patio.

I follow him out and take in the set up. The focal point of the area is a really nice in-ground pool, and to the side is a built-in grill. We each take a seat on a couple lounge chairs set off to the other side. As soon as we're seated, we both say, "I'm sorry." Then we both laugh.

Trevor speaks first. "I'm sorry, Sara. I'm sorry for pushing you for more when I knew you couldn't give it. I was selfish. I wasn't thinking about your job, your life, or the kids. I mean, I was, but I wasn't. I just assumed you could have all those same things here. I was wrong."

"I'm sorry for pushing you away," I tell him. "I was scared. I was scared of what I felt for you the minute I met you. I kept trying to talk myself out of spending time with you. I knew it would end, and when it did, I would be in too deep. I did what I do best, and I reacted. I pushed you away instead of talking about it, instead of trying to compromise. I'm so used to doing things on my own, Trevor. I'm so sorry."

"So were you?" he asks quietly.

"Was I what?" I look at him, puzzled.

His forearms are resting on his thighs, his hands are clasped together, and he's not looking at me. He's looking down at his sneakers. "Were you in too deep when it ended?" he finally says.

"I was," I admit. "I still am."

His head lifts up and his eyes meet mine. He's seeking the truth in my words. I can tell the moment he finds it because he leans forward, closing the three foot gap between us. Taking my face in his hands, he crashes his mouth against mine. His tongue taps the seam of my lips and I open for him. We both moan at the long lost contact. My hands are in his hair, his are still on my face, as we explore each other for the first time in months.

When he finally pulls away, he whispers "Me too."

"What does this mean?" I ask, afraid of what he'll say...afraid of what he won't say...

"It means we try," he says, leaning his forehead against mine. His hands are still framing my face, and I don't want him to ever let go.

"It's not going to be easy." All my trepidations are back in full force, as if they'd never left. How are we going to make this work?

"No, it's not. But there's no reason I can't go back and forth for a while. I don't need to be here all the time."

I'm nervous because it still feels like we're putting off the inevitable. Sure, a temporary long distance relationship situation is doable. But what about forever? We can't do long distance forever. I think back to the first few days after Trevor left and how awful it was missing him. I can't imagine how much worse that feeling will get once we get in even deeper.

"Hey," he says, rubbing his thumbs against my cheeks. I look into his eyes. "Stop thinking so hard. We'll figure this out, Sara. I promise. Do you trust me?"

As I stare deep into his eyes, I realize that I do. I do trust him. I smile and nod in response. His answering smile lights up his eyes, and he kisses me again. I wrap my arms around his neck and press my body against his, wanting to feel as much of him as I possibly can. But it's awkward in this seated position. He gets it, though, and moves to crawl on top of me as I lie back in the lounger. My knees are bent and straddling his thighs, and I can feel the delicious friction between my legs—something else I'd longed for in his absence.

When I grind myself against him, he breaks the kiss, resting his forehead against mine with a sigh. "Yeah...so we probably shouldn't get too excited on the patio."

I feel my cheeks heat, and I look towards the house to see if anyone caught our display. Thankfully, no one is around.

"You're probably right. Alex and Chase have been gone for a while with the kids, they'll probably be back soon."

Trevor makes a move to get up, but I haven't unlocked my legs from his waist or my arms from his neck. "A little help here?" he laughs.

I laugh with him for a moment then sober up. "I don't want to let go of you. I missed you so much."

He sighs and sits up, taking me with him since I'm still strapped onto his chest like one of those strappy baby carriers. He wraps his strong arms around me and kisses my temple. "I missed you, too," he whispers. A few tears creep out of my eyes and run down my cheeks. He kisses those away, too. "Everything is going to be okay. I'm not going to let you go this time."

I sniffle and nod my head against his shoulder.

He softly laughs. "Do I need to carry you inside?"

"Maybe," I giggle. "Do you think we can just sit out here together for a minute? Just the two of us?"

"Of course."

I finally release my death grip, and he adjusts us so we're laying side-by-side. The lounge chair is narrow, so I'm nestled tightly against him, from head to toe. Not that I'm complaining. If we were lying on an empty beach I'd still want to be this close to him. He has his arms wrapped around me, holding me close, and my head is resting on his firm bicep.

"So what do you think is going to happen with Nora?" he asks after a minute.

I sigh, not wanting to talk about my sister. But that's what normal couples do. They talk about everything—the good, the bad, and the ugly.

"I don't really know. Her chance at custody of the kids is shot, though. The judge was very adamant that this was her only chance. She had to make these visits count. Once he gets word that she left the county with them and abandoned them in a seedy motel..."

"It's a shame," Trevor says.

"It is. They're such amazing kids. I will never understand why she couldn't put them first, for once. Why was everything more important than them?"

"They're amazing kids because of you, Sara. Because you raised them and took care of them. You turned them into the perfect little people they are. They're lucky to have you. Yeah, it sucks they didn't have their birth mother, and they may call you auntie, but you're their mom in every sense of the word. They're happy. They know love. That's what matters. You can worry and wonder about the 'what ifs,' but the truth is...it's just not worth your time. You tried. You gave Nora the benefit of the doubt. She gave it all up. She gave them up. You'll only kill yourself trying to figure out why she did what she did."

I nod, knowing he's right, and a few more tears escape. I'm not sure I've ever had someone believe in me the way he does.

"So what else have I missed?" he asks, sweetly changing the subject.

I tell him about the rest of our summer and the twins entering the first grade. Apparently they had shared some of their experiences with him last night, but we laugh together at their antics anyway, particularly the story of when Georgie brought a dried up sand crab to school and scared half the female students. He tells me about their time in the studio and talks about some of the tracks that will be on the new album. He asks me to be his date to Ally's wedding, and of course, I agree.

Being here in his arms...it feels so right and so perfect.

I never want this moment to end.

Chapter Forty-Seven

Trevor

Later in the evening, the adults are sitting around the fire pit on the patio. Since it's Columbus Day weekend, the kids don't have school tomorrow, so Sara decided to stay another night. Joey and Evie joined us with Max, and the kids all wore each other out earlier. They're currently passed out in the living room, in the blanket fort Alex helped them build. Sara is cuddled into my side, laughing at something Ally just said.

Things couldn't be any better.

"So when are you headed back?" Evie asks Sara.

"I have to go back tomorrow, the kids have school on Tuesday."

"What are you going to do about your car?" Ally asks.

"I'm going to drive them back," I say.

Sara looks up at me. "But I need a car to drive."

"You can drive mine."

"How are you going to get home if I have your car? And how will I get my car back?" Her eyebrows scrunch together as she tries to figure it out.

"Alex can drive the Jeep out, and I'll take him home."

She nods in understanding.

"They said the car will take a couple days," Alex chimes in.

Sara looks up at me with concern. "Is that okay? Can you be gone that long? I can rent a car, Trevor. You don't have to drive me."

I shake my head. "No, my girl isn't renting a car when I can drive her."

Her cheeks redden, and she tucks her face back into my side. I kiss the top of her head and look up at my brother, sister, and friends...my family. They're all smiling, obviously pleased with the turn of events between Sara and me.

Well, now is as good a time as any.

"Alex, why don't you drive the Jeep out in a few weeks." Everyone's eyes widen at my words, and Sara pulls away to look up at me.

"A few weeks?" she asks quietly.

"Maybe more. If that's alright with you," I tell her.

She looks at me carefully, trying to decipher my meaning. "But aren't you recording?"

"I finished up my part."

"But your family is here."

I look around, taking in the faces of my loved ones glowing in the firelight. Alex and Joey share the same shit-eating grin they always seem to wear. Chase nods at me with a small, but meaningful, smile. Evie smiles and give me a thumbs up. And Ally wipes a tear from her eye as she cuddles into Chase's side, giving me an approving smile as well.

"Yeah, they are." I say, answering Sara's question and looking into her beautiful blue eyes. "But you're not. And right now...you're where I want to be...where I need to be."

"But what if you get sick of me? The kids?"

"I won't."

"But what if you do?"

I roll my eyes. "Then I'll leave."

Her eyes narrow. "Trevor—"

"Sara. We said we'd try. We can't try with more than 300 miles between us."

She frowns, and I can tell she's trying to think of some logical reason why this doesn't make sense.

To hell with that. I don't let her say another word. I tilt my head forward and press my lips to hers. God, I love kissing her. I love...her. Deepening the kiss, I'm vaguely aware that my family is front and center to our display of affection, but I don't care. But Sara does, she pulls away and smiles shyly. Her blush is irresistible, and I just want to kiss her again.

Before I can she holds her hand up. "Whoa there, Tiger. Calm it down now."

Everyone laughs, and I put my arm around her shoulder, pulling her back into my side where she belongs.

Right beside me.

***

The next morning, I load the bags I hastily packed into the back of my Land Rover. Sara is herding the twins, and everyone is standing in the driveway, waiting to bid us farewell or bon voyage or whatever it is people do when one of their loved ones is going away for a few weeks.

Sara and the twins make their way down the line, hugging everyone and laughing at whatever silly things Alex is saying. She gives me a kiss on the cheek as she walks passed me to load the kids in the car.

"We'll see you real soon," Joey says as he gives me a hug. I nod in response, getting a little choked up.

"You take good care of her and those kids," Evie warns, kissing me on the cheek.

"I will," I promise.

I squat down and give Max a fist-bump. "I'll see you soon, kid."

"Bye, Uncle Twevow," he says around the fingers in his mouth. I hug him, then tickle his side to lighten my mood.

Alex is next, and I then realize how much this sucks. Joey has Evie, Ally has Chase, but who does Alex have? Alex reads my expression and says, "Don't worry about me, brother. I've got a few ladies waiting in the wings. I won't be lonely long."

My brother, the man-whore, ladies and gentlemen. I laugh and wrap him my arms around him and squeeze until he's laughing through his gasps for breath...all the while I'm fighting back the tears that threaten to spill. The lump in my throat is killing me. "I'll see you in a few weeks."

Chase, always the silent one, gives me a hug with a manly pat on the back. "Later, brother."

"Take care of her," I tell him, tipping my head towards Ally.

"You don't even have to ask." I nod, knowing that he will...knowing that I really didn't have to ask.

Ally damn near breaks my resolve with the tears pouring down her face. "I love you, big brother," she says as she launches herself into my arms.

"I love you, too, kid."

"I'm so happy for you," she mumbles into my shirt. "You deserve this," she says as she pulls away, her hands still holding my arms. "You deserve to be happy, too."

"Thanks, Al. Take care of him," I say, gesturing to Chase. She smiles as she steps back and takes his hand.

"Always."

"Take care of him, too," I say, pointing over to Alex.

"I don't need no taking care of!" he shouts, making us all laugh and breaking the depressing mood.

"I'll see you all soon," I say, giving one last glance down the line.

They all call out their goodbyes as I walk around the SUV and get into the driver's seat. Once inside I buckle my seat belt, adjust the mirrors, and sigh. Sara reaches over the console and squeezes my hand.

I look into her eyes and smile. This is what my future holds. Sara and those two awesome little monsters in the back seat, currently watching some animated flick on the built-in DVD player.

I turn on the engine, and then, giving one last wave to my family, pull out of the driveway and into the street.

I take Sara's hand and lift it to my lips, pressing a soft kiss on her palm. She smiles at me and I smile back.

"You sure about this?" she asks me, for the eight hundredth time in the last twelve hours.

I squeeze her hand and nod. "Let's go home."

The End.

Acknowledgements

A big thank you to all the readers out there. Without you, authors wouldn't write and, I can really only speak for myself here, but if I couldn't write, I'd probably lose my mind with all the stories floating around in it. Thank you to my family and friends for their support. I appreciate you all so much. A special thank you to my niece Madeline for helping me to recollect our vacation to the Outer Banks. Thank you to my alpha reader, LaDonna. I appreciate your feedback in alpha and beta so much. You gave me the encouragement I needed in the beginning to keep going. Big thanks to my beta readers: Ginni, Amanda, Heather, and Melissa for your feedback and endless support. Melissa, thank you for the quotes! I am not kidding when I say you have a gift. Thank you Aimee, my editor, for all your hard work and support. I appreciate what you've done for me so much. Natasha, my proofreader, for helping put the finishing touches on this book. Your role is last, but definitely not least. I'm sure a lot of people appreciate your keen eye! Thank you to Cassy at Pink Ink Designs for the beautiful cover design. You've done amazing work on this and other projects for me and I'm looking forward to working with you again and again and again in the future. Thank you to all the bloggers participating in the blog activities and pimping the heck out of my books! You are all amazing and I wish I could hug each and every one of you. Thank you to Jennifer's

Chapter Chicks for being my sounding board. You have no idea what a relief it is to have a group of readers and friends to bounce ideas off of and be a little crazy with. I appreciate you all so much.

About the Author

Jennifer lives in South Carolina with her husband and their three fur-kids. She is in grad school, pursuing a Masters in Psychology for Clinical Counseling. When she is not at work or taking classes, she is either reading or writing. Books have always been her passion. She also enjoys spending time with her family, traveling to new places, and music.

Connect With Me

Email: jenniferlallenauthor@gmail.com

Website: www.jenniferlallenauthor.com

Facebook: www.facebook.com/jallenauthor

Twitter: https://twitter.com/AuthorJenniferA

Mailing List:
https://tinyletter.com/JenniferLAllenAuthor

Books by
Jennifer L. Allen

Our Moon: JACT Book One
Hearts in the Sand: JACT Book Two

Change of Heart